Bra

Branded

PAUL WHEELAHAN

A Black Horse Western

ROBERT HALE · LONDON

First published in Great Britain 2000

ISBN 0 7090 6747 X

Robert Hale Limited
Clerkenwell House
Clerkenwell Green
London EC1R 0HT

Typeset by
Derek Doyle & Associates, Liverpool.
Printed and bound in Great Britain by
The Cromwell Press

1

Man from Rio Hondo

The long day was dying when the group loafing on the porch of Arroyo's biggest saloon suddenly broke off their desultory conversation to stare east.

A mile out along the trail something was emerging from the eternal dust hazing the Pecos side of town.

Rider coming in off the desert by the looks.

This was enough to command the full attention of the six-man membership of the Ten Bar's sit-and-spit club, for rarely did anybody simply arrive in bleak Arroyo; its isolation and reputation guaranteed against that.

Still, there was no law saying any man wasn't free to push his horse across fifty waterless miles of sand and mesquite to reach this squalid outpost of desolation here in the bleak heart of New Mexico's northern desert lands, providing his nerve was good and his cayuse was up to it.

Heads nodded as the dust-shrouded figures took shape. Someone drifting in right enough. Tall man leading a big grulla horse, and it seemed the horse was favoring its off side hind foot some.

'Yup, lame hoss,' muttered the bald-headed oldster, as grizzled, gray and gnarled as a horned lizard. 'Least we know why this one's come our way, boys.'

In Arroyo, whether it be on the very last day of the sweltering Indian summer, like today, or midnight in midwinter, it was always good to know who or what it might be drifting in, just in case.

'A runner, you figure?' speculated a blocky man with the punched-in face of a brawler. By and large, most everybody who came to Arroyo was running from something.

'Or then it jest might be a chaser, Jesse,' a loser with black eye-patch speculated mischievously. He raised the patch from the hollow eye socket as though to enhance his vision – a party trick he had. He nodded. 'Y'know, mebbe I can see a badge at that.'

Bad taste had to be pretty poor before it offended your friends at the good old Ten Bar. This lawman 'joke' managed it. Hard faces glared at One Eye, unamused, then went back to studying the newcomer, now making his way across the old plank-bridge slung across the hook in dust-dry Fork Creek.

He came on with a long, tireless stride, a tall and rangy man of around thirty. Wide of shoulder and lean of hip, his level gray eyes cut to the deck-chair loafers with a challenging gleam as he drew abreast of the saloon before halting, standing in dust up to his spurs.

'You still got a livery here?' His tone was halfway between polite and brusque.

He looked beat, they saw plainly now. Unshaven, dust-coated and wind-burnt, he'd plainly been on foot for quite a spell, crossing one of the harshest stretches of real estate in the country. And yet he appeared more formidable than weary, while the revolver he wore strapped to his right thigh looked as if it fitted there real comfortable.

Even so, in that brief moment of mutual appraisal, it was less the man's appearance than his words that aroused their curiosity.

Had this beat-up desert dude actually employed the word 'still'? Like, maybe he'd been here before?

They claimed that self-styled sage Old Elijah was half cracked and way past it after fifty years on the Furnace. Yet as was often the case with this clannish bunch of saloon lizards and free-drink scroungers, the oldster yet again proved himself the sharpest of them all as he creaked forward in his sun-faded canvas chair to point an unsteady finger at the figure in the street.

'By dab and tarnation!' he croaked, licking dry lips. 'It cain't be . . . but ah reckon it is.' He raised his voice. 'You're him, ain't you, son? Kindersley's man. . . .' He paused, searching through his memory file for a name. He snapped his fingers. 'Gannon. You thet Gannon feller, ain't thet so?'

'Don't fret, I'll find it myself,' was all the reply he drew. And the stranger was on his way again, leading his limping horse off into the canyon of sagging falsefronts, creaking doorways and tumbleweed alleyways, braving the suspicious stares of a town about ready to lie down.

'What'd you jest say, you old goat?' demanded a black-bearded felon with a jaw like a wolf trap. 'Gannon? Who in hail he?'

'It's Gannon is who, you idjut!' Animated now, Old Elijah hopped up and gesticulated. 'Is that poor brain of your'n so addled you don't recall when Gannon come to town?'

'Glory, Gannon!' exclaimed the storekeeper, eyes wide as he too jumped erect to gape after the receding tall figure. 'B'God, it sure enough looks like that *hombre* now you come to say, old man. But . . . surely he daid? Didn't we figger he was gonna croak for sure when them lawdogs was done with him that night?'

'So we figgered when he rode out all shot to hell, but he sure looks live enough to me,' replied the oldster, smugly self-satisfied now as he spat and scratched. Then he shook his head. 'But man, that boy sure has changed in the space of a year. Scarce recognized him, I never.'

A one-armed sneak thief gasped, 'A year? You mean to say it's that long ago since them possemen from the Sangres durn near shot this here town to doll rags?'

It was indeed. A full year and more now. And Cole Gannon, former Sangre de Cristo rancher, branded killer, could feel the full weight of every day and hour of that lonesome time heavy upon him now as he made his way to the center of town, still the focus of every eye as he searched for the livery he knew to be here someplace.

The men in the street hadn't placed him as yet and their stares reflected a mix of hostility and curiosity. This didn't faze him; he expected nothing less. Arroyo was that kind of town. And just like any honest man who'd ever visited this pest-hole for whatever reason, there was no way he'd have ever come back but for the stone-bruised hoof that had forced him to come in off the Furnace, thus interrupting his long journey home to the Sangre de Cristo.

Memory bit like a rabid dog as he approached the geographical centerpoint of Arroyo-on-the-Fork, the large circular pool of the ornamental fountain, which was eternally bone-dry and littered with rubble. Close by the fountain, the unpainted gallery of the sagging hotel was liberally scarred by bullet holes both new and old. Carved lintels overhung weathered doorways; flower-beds in a crevice between two leaning buildings were clogged with drifting sand.

On the opposite side of the waterless fountain stood the burnt-out skeleton of the law office that had been unoccupied for a decade, and a tiny bat-infested church which had been closed down even longer.

And just a short distance further on, the livery.

The rush of emotion that gripped him as he stared at this building through the fading light was totally unexpected. He wasn't prepared for it. Life had honed this fugitive hard, almost beyond feeling, or so he'd thought. Yet this jolt of shock along with the stab of remembered pain which gripped his body where two bullets had drilled into him during that night of red violence, were almost innocuous compared with his reaction, when upon circling the fountain he found himself confronting the barn door.

Against the fall of night the Arroyo Feed and Grain Barn thrust its log-and-daub shoulder above him, its shabby old walls rising dark and scarred from out of the dust. Directly overhead loomed the heavy oak beam which served as a hoist for bales of hay stored in the loft, at eye level the door itself, fashioned from hickory and pinewood with rusted iron hasps and a busted padlock.

The town, the citizens and the buildings – even the sight of the barn itself – hadn't really affected him. But the door was something different, so different in truth, that it caused the hair on the back of his neck to lift and saw his fingers instinctively stray to his gunbutt.

He couldn't take his eyes off it.

It had never crossed his mind that they mightn't have repaired the damage following that night of mayhem.

It should have.

In Arroyo, they never got to fix anything – leaking roofs, broken hearts, busted doorways – anything.

Unchanged since that night when Cole Gannon, rancher, solid citizen and branded killer had come to this hell-hole running like a coyote hunted by a relay of hound dogs, this unpainted and sagging entryway to the old barn looked exactly the same to his haggard eye. Splintered, sagging, liberally pocked with vicious bullet holes and stained by a vast brownish smear across its lower half of what he knew to be blood.

His blood.

Gannon sagged against the horse's sweating neck

and passed a hand over his eyes as memory went clicking back.

They were closing in.

He'd punched a slug through a deputy's thigh back by the saloon, and blown a posseman's fat mare out from underneath him in the alley opposite the Arroyo General Store. Yet stumbling round the ornamental fountain in the smoke-choked gloom with pain gripping his back and a near-empty Colt .45 in his fist, Gannon, who'd figured he might stand at least half a chance of making it to that alley by the livery, suddenly jerked to a halt with a curse hissing through locked teeth.

Two shadowy figures had materialized from the hazy gloom enshrouding the livery stables; at the same instant a third man burst into view on the upper gallery of Lady Kate's opposite, bawling orders at the top of his lungs.

'Finish him off, you cretins. Can't you see he's hit? Cut him down! Kill him!'

Kindersley's voice. Unmistakably, chillingly, that was the deep-chested roar of Sheriff Boyd Kindersley of Tarryall, possemaster, crook, and the man entirely responsible for the running man's desperate situation.

Gannon flung himself low beneath the cover of the fountain's cracked wall a split second before the six-gunners before him opened fire thunderously, almost but not quite drowning out the lawman's booming voice.

Even in that hair-raising moment with his life hanging by a thread and the air filled with flying bullets, Cole Gannon could still scarce believe it had all happened – the death of his friend, the incredible accusations by the sheriff, the flight, the posse, the sixty miles of pursuit from the Sangre de Cristo to this hell-hole and his final desperate facedown with misguided men who wanted to kill him.

No nightmare could ever be this bad. So it had to be real. Therefore he must go on acting accordingly.

Kill or be killed.

It was this exact moment of decision that saw Cole Gannon, law-abiding rancher and good citizen, cease to exist. In his stead stood a dangerous man with ice in his veins and remorseless purpose in every movement as he fingered fresh shells into a blued-steel gun chamber, sucked in a huge breath and erupted from cover in full attack mode, trigger-finger working overtime.

His unexpected onslaught caught the pair by the livery in the open. Zigzagging as he came on, Gannon continued firing and the possemen threw themselves full length with slugs ripping up the dust around their rolling bodies. But gunshots from another quarter whistled close, and Gannon was forced to slew violently sideways, managing to get the reassuring solidness of the old barn door against his back. His gun whipped up and loosed two shots at the silhouette of the big figure up on the balcony, and this average shooter never used his gun better.

Kindersley went down with a clatter, crashing heavily against the railing, threatening to smash his way through it with the bulk of his big body.

Remorseless now, Gannon was taking aim and looking to finish off his man when the sprawled deputies got their guns working again, and the sudden pain ripping through his flank caused him to drop to one knee. Through a stinging haze of sweat, the blurred faces of Kindersley's men resembled those of feral beasts, yellow-eyed and snarling.

He was one sick rancher as he jerked off another shot. His aim was lousy. He was too bullet shocked to expect any better. Yet his slug ripped into the barn wall, ricocheted off with a vicious whine of sound and smacked into the nearer gunman's arm with a meaty thud. The man convulsed in agony and slewed off balance into his companion, jolting the weapon from his hand.

It was the faintest sliver of a chance; one narrow window of opportunity.

Gannon grabbed it.

Heaving himself upright, his bloodied back still against the door, he gulped down a huge lungful of air then went plunging for the darkened maw of the alleyway, the precious darkness.

Legs pumping, hostile sounds reaching him in errant waves, he was within feet of the alley-mouth when a figure lunged from it unexpectedly before him. The quiet rancher reacted savagely. One blow of his gunbarrel felled the figure at his feet, and bones crunched as Gannon stamped on the upturned face to launch himself into a headlong dive that took him into the blackness, the warlike sounds from the street immediately dimmed by the high walls.

Only one voice carried clearly, a voice laced with pain and rage. 'Five hundred to the man who stops him!' Kindersley sounded almost hysterical. 'A thousand!'

But Gannon was flying now. A quick sprint, the rapid tattoo of boot heels on hard-packed earth, saw him swoop round a sharp corner to bring him into a short side-street where he glimpsed a big bay horse fighting its tether at a hitch rail.

One enormous bound saw the badly wounded man fill leather and dig with steel. The rush of cold night air against his face was a benediction as he went streaking away to leave the gunfire, the burning hotel and the howls of fury receding in his wake: 'Gannon! Gannon's gettin' away. . . .'

'Gannon, hey, Gannon, you all right, man?'

He blinked, and the blurring outlines of unpainted buildings whirling by as he lay bleeding across the neck of a racing horse all faded abruptly to give way to the hard-edged reality of daylight, the solid reality of the sturdy old barn and the leathered face before him.

It was the liveryman.

'Huh?' he grunted. Then shook his head in disbelief and annoyance, amazed that he could have allowed himself to be carried away like that. After all, it was only a lousy door. 'Of course I'm all right,' he snapped, fingering back his hat as he glanced around. 'Why wouldn't I be?'

He was not a man given to flights of fancy, but the sheer impact of finding himself back on this exact spot which seemed to evoke everything evil that had befallen him the previous year, had proven overwhelming even for this stoic survivor. He could admit it now that he seemed to understand it.

'Sorry,' the towner said. 'Just thought you looked

a little peaked is all.' He glanced past him and nodded. 'It's all right, boys, nothin' to worry about, I guess. He's okay.'

Gannon whirled. Upwards of twenty towners were now clustered round the fountain where he'd been alone before. Their stares were different now, some beginning to smile amiably and admiringly, the old-timer from the Ten Bar even saluting and nodding like they were old buddies.

'Dang glad to see you back with us and still alive and kickin', Gannon. We all figgered you was gonna croak that night you lit out of here splashin' blood all over the street like you was fixed on repaintin' it.'

'And leavin' all them stove-up lawdogs in his dust, layin' round and moanin' something pitiful,' another said with relish. 'Don't fergit them, old man.'

Gannon took a backward step as understanding hit.

He didn't know any of these people from Adam, and yet they were appearing from everywhere now to encircle him admiringly, dirty, diseased and dangerous-looking to a man or woman, yet ogling him as though he were an old friend or the prodigal son returned to Arroyo's grimy bosom.

Or even a hero.

He swung on the liveryman, who now smiled fawningly. 'This is a big day for us, Mr Gannon.' The man's sweeping gesture encompassed fountain, saloon, hotel and barn. 'You comin' back, that is. Guess scarce a day goes by we don't talk about the night the posse chased you down here . . . and how you dusted 'em off and durn nigh done for that top-lofty scumdog of a high sheriff.' He doffed his sorry Stetson and swung it above his head. 'Ain't this so, folks? Ain't Mr Gannon our ever-lovin' champeen?'

A ragged cheer rose in the evening air, startling little bull bats into harried flight from the belfry of the ruined old church opposite. They were lauding him, and Cole Gannon was repulsed. They seemed to regard him as one of their own. Certainly he'd fought it out here with certified lawmen that night – Arroyo's natural enemies – but this didn't make him any sort of desperado or outlaw. Not in his own eyes at least, even if there might be still fading Wanted dodgers all over the high country offering $500 for 'killer' Cole Gannon, dead or alive.

Twelve months on from that brutal night, one whole year spent in exile along the Rio Hondo, he was still just Cole Gannon, cowman and proud New Mexican. Nothing more.

And what such man would not be offended to find himself held up as some kind of idol by the dregs of the desert.

'My horse picked up a stone-bruise,' he said stiffly, turning his back on the rapidly swelling crowd. 'I want to trade him or rent another to get me where I'm going—'

'Got the very animal you want,' the liveryman cut in. 'And it's your'n for as long as you want it, Mr Gannon. Free of charge. Your money ain't no good in Arroyo, by Lawdy Lord.' His face suffused with pleasure. 'Y'know, one of them yellow-dog deputies you plugged was laid up here for five weeks, and big Kindersley hisself is still limpin' from the slug you nailed into his leg, so we hear tell.' He bowed and gestured flamboyantly towards his livery. 'After you, Mr Gannon, sir, after you.'

The man was as good as his word. The sturdy buckskin gelding was exactly the sort of horse Gannon needed to tackle that final sixty miles and make up for the time he'd lost detouring here to the armpit of Furnace Desert.

His business in Fall River County couldn't wait. Dusk was falling fast and the street was still crowded when he rode the buckskin from the stables, leading the grulla. They cheered again but Gannon remained stony faced as he nodded stiffly at the liveryman. Sure, he was grateful, but resentment was stronger.

'Much obliged,' he managed to get out. He raised his voice, 'Make way, I'm running short of time.'

'Where you headin', son?' called the graybeard. 'North, huh? Goin' back for another crack at them polecats that nigh done fer you, I guess? Dunno 'bout the others, but you won't find thet Kindersley hard to find. They say he's ridin' higher'n ever these days, the big mucker. Well, we'll all be rootin' for you, young feller, you can bet on that.'

'Give Kindersley one from us, Gannon!' shouted another, shaking a fist. 'He has to be the easiest man to hate that ever come to this town. So let's send the man on his way right, boys. Gannon! Gannon! Gannon!'

Eagerly they took up the chant, but Gannon made no response as he touched up the buckskin to force his way through grinning faces and clutching hands. They loved him. And nothing could have made him feel worse. Yet as street gave way to trail beneath him and he urged the horses into a run for the plank bridge, with distant lightning flickering in the darkening sky, Gannon turned just once to glance back and felt reality hit home hard.

They were right about him, he realized.

Leaving Rio Hondo, he'd convinced himself he was heading home for the noblest of reasons, to help out old friends.

But rough and ready Arroyo had smelt him out. They were convinced he was on a delayed mission of revenge against Sheriff Boyd Kindersley. They just could be right, he saw now.

For he was a realist, and reality suggested strongly he must again clash with the man who'd wrecked his life and branded him killer. So where did he get off taking the moral high ground? Might not whatever lay ahead of him in the Sangres force him to act just like the vengeance-hunting desperado the citizens of Arroyo mistook him for?

'The hell it will!' he vowed, the sudden sound of his voice causing the buckskin to toggle its ears. Angrily he kicked the horse into a run and rode into the coming storm.

2
I am the Law

In the solid oak guarding the foot of the pass a drowsing hawk suddenly cocked its head and came fully alert. Rising up on the bough, it flexed handsome wings, spreading them wide. Then, launching itself into space it flapped away from its perch and began to climb.

The predator was a hundred feet above the pines, elms and firs of the border between the rolling rangelands of the High T and Lazy Y spreads, when the noise that had startled it sounded clearer now: the swift stutter of wheels and hoofbeats drawing rapidly closer along the hard-packed trail.

The buckboard burst into sight abruptly to go rushing by the oak heading for the graceful bend leading downslope to the main Tarryall trail.

It was a standard ranch rig with cut-under front gear, drawn by a slab-flanked bay horse, the only thing unusual about it being that the driver was a woman.

Fall River County was all ranch, timber and mining country up here high above the plains where the winters were long and the life tolerably harsh. As a consequence, this upper range of the Nacimientos in the Sangres was manifestly masculine in both population and attitudes.

Which bothered Tessa Dorling not one iota.

Mistress of the Lazy Y, which she had just left, and daughter of Perce Dorling, who didn't get around much anymore, Tessa had been holding down a full-time man's job and travelling freely about the high county just as men did for as long as the Dorlings had been ranching up here, more so than ever since losing her brother under violent circumstances a year earlier.

Of course these emancipated attitudes didn't impress everybody, and Tessa could trigger off a virtual brushfire of tongue-wagging and head-shaking whenever the more genteel ladies of Tarryall might observe her rushing by in the ranch rig, or worse, stopping off for a cold beer at the saloon if the day was hot.

Her critics liked to imply she was less than feminine, but the number of admirers lithe Tessa managed to attract despite her seeming indifference to menfolk in general tended to silence her critics, leaving her free to do just about as she liked.

But ranch life in the mountains, whether you happened to be a wealthy cattle baron and business tycoon like Slater Whitney, or simply ran a modest double quarter section like the Lazy Y, was always demanding and never more so than whenever the rustlers were busy. And rustling was the ugly business which was taking Tessa to town on what might be one of the last snow-free days of the changing season.

Another twenty head had been run off the Lazy Y last night, while the mighty High T continued to lose quality stock at an alarming rate, as had been the case for far too long. It was hard to understand how Sheriff Kindersley, so impressively efficient and successful in virtually every other area of his jurisdiction, could continue to dismally fail in his efforts to haul the cow thieves responsible up before Judge Murdoch. Of course most county folk were too intimidated by their sheriff to complain too vigorously on the matter, but just the way Tessa was driving headlong for Tarryall suggested strongly that the kid gloves would be off when she and the lawman faced off.

Tessa found the big, spacious law office, with its pine floors and walls and wide windows overlooking Pawnee Street, deserted but for one deputy when she arrived thirty minutes later. The raw-boned young man was busy sweeping out the cells but stopped smartly enough when her slender shadow fell through his doorway.

'Why, morning, Miss Tessa,' he grinned, stowing the broom and rubbing his sleeve across his badge. 'What brings you in this early in the day?' He was one of the young blades of the town who considered this lath-slim young woman about as feminine and desirable as they came, regardless of what the old biddies of the town might think to the contrary. 'Sheriff's on patrol but if I can be of service, er, ma'am?'

'You don't have to ma'am me, Deputy, I'm not as

old as you are.' She stood tapping her foot and glancing round impatiently, posters of wanted hellions returning her gaze from immaculate walls. She stopped tapping when her gaze focused on the dodger portraying a strong and clean-cut face which to her eyes seemed wildly out of place amongst bearded ruffians and stone-eyed killers. 'And just how long is that picture of Cole Gannon going to remain up there, might I enquire, Deputy?'

The man reddened. 'Shucks, ma'am – I mean, Miss Tessa—'

'Never mind,' she cut in brusquely. 'I suppose there's no point in Sheriff Kindersley bringing false accusations against a man unless he is prepared to pursue it to the bitter end, is there?'

The deputy concentrated on buffing his star again. He wouldn't touch that one with a barge pole. You didn't raise the Gannon affair with Tessa Dorling unless you enjoyed a good tongue lashing.

The woman turned her back to the dodgers. Tall and dagger-slim in faded denim pants and worn leather jacket, there was no question in the deputy's mind she was the office's most attractive visitor since . . . well, since the last time she came in to tell his superior off, he supposed.

She said, 'He's on patrol, you say?'

'Just round town, Tessa. Afoot, that is.'

'Not out searching for the rustlers who ran twenty cows off my place last night then?'

'Er, no, ma'am. But goldurn it all I just cain't believe the Lazy Y got hit again!'

'Indeed. Again.' She swung for the door but paused with a frown. 'Where are the other deputies?

It seems they are never about when I come to town these days.'

'Shucks, I'm just like the janitor hereabouts these days. I wouldn't know where—'

'Never mind. Where might I find the sheriff?'

Either at the council chambers, the courthouse with the judge or maybe uptown at the freight depot, she was told. She left, declining his offer of coffee so brusquely that the young deputy was left trying to decide whether she was just in a real bad mood, or if maybe he wasn't half the dashing buck he imagined himself to be.

Tarryall was a sizeable town by mountain standards, being the center of trade, commerce and law for over one third of the county. There was a heavy rumble of wagon traffic over echoing Beaver River bridge directly beyond which stood the imposing white courthouse and the adjacent council chambers building with its copper cupola gleaming dully like a dragon's head in the pallid sunlight.

She didn't find the sheriff at either place, but did spy a familiar figure lighting up a fat cigar as he emerged from the courthouse. She approached as Judge Cletus Murdoch exhaled a huge gust of smoke, his red-lidded eyes twinkling with interest the moment they met hers.

'Ahh, the sylvan beauty of the piney woods,' he intoned fruitily, a decaying old jurist who loved the sound of his own voice almost as much as he did good tobacco and blended bourbon. He doffed his black hat and held it against his string tie, boiled white shirt and black vest. 'My dear Miss Dorling, to what do we decadent town dwellers owe the honor of your stirring Amazonian presence, pray?'

Tessa half smiled. She liked the presiding justice of the 23rd District Court of northern New Mexico even if not everyone shared her feelings. Some claimed Murdoch was corrupt and too much in the sheriff's pocket; most everyone agreed he was an alcoholic. She supposed she supported both contentions. Yet she still liked him. He did have manners when he chose to use them. Which made him a rarity here.

'I'm looking for Sheriff Kindersley, Judge Murdoch.'

'Alas! For a fleeting moment I thought it may have been my estimable self you were seeking, my bucolic beauty.' He held up a silencing hand as she made to reply. 'No, no need to state the obvious. I'll readily concede I may be eons too old for you, but I'd argue the case before the Supreme Court itself that you are in no way too young for me.' He jammed his cigar between yellowed teeth and turned serious, his customary demeanor. 'The sheriff was here but left to go on to the depot. Anything I might assist you with, girl?'

'Not unless you're fitter than you look, Judge. I'm looking for somebody to chase cow thieves for me.'

'Not again?'

'I'm afraid so. Twenty head last night.'

Murdoch's face was wreathed in smoke as he exhaled through flaring nostrils.

'Damnation! What's the big attraction about Lazy Y cows anyway? No offence, my dear, but I'd never sink my teeth into one of your stringy steers while ever there was a haunch of prime, grain-fed beef to be had anywhere in the county. This recent spate of raids on your place just doesn't make one scintilla of sense, damned if it does.'

Which was exactly what Tessa Dorling told Sheriff Kindersley when she finally ran him to earth two blocks north on upper Pawnee at the sprawling Whitney freight depot and commission house.

The lawman made no attempt to disguise his reluctance to be dragged away from the great sturdy warehouses with their mazes of offices, corridors and loading landings, the rich scents of tobacco and bacon, the sack piles and barrels and bins of corn, barley and oats that comprised this, the commercial heart of his town.

Eventually he gave ground, though was obviously anything but pleased as the couple made their way along a gloomy passageway to emerge on to a quiet, empty landing where they might talk in private.

'Well, let's hear about your incident, Tessa,' he sighed, 'or can I guess the details, the *modus operandi*? Let's see . . . night strike, nobody saw anything, no leads. Is that about it?'

Tessa's lips pursed as she studied the big man with the brass star. The two simply didn't get along. She had always found Boyd Kindersley arrogant and antagonistic, and this seemed to be his general demeanor so far as the 'little people' of the county were concerned. With the Slater Whitneys or the mining and lumber bosses it was very different. Kindersley had always been tight with these shakers and movers, although was now reputedly at odds with Slater Whitney due to his uncharacteristic failure to stem the rustling raids that had been costing the

High T dearly all year. Even so, he still commanded more than enough electoral support from the majority of the rich and powerful of the county to guarantee he got himself voted back in year after year despite a general falling off of popularity since the heady days when he had tamed a once wild Tarryall.

'It's amazing, Sheriff,' she said at length. 'You seem to know everything about that incident.' She paused deliberately. 'Except for what happened to my stolen stock, that is. You didn't solve that mystery the last time we were robbed, or the time before that, did you? Am I to believe that the next time we're raided, and I'm sure we will be, you'll know every little thing except what counts most?'

Kindersley flushed at her sarcasm, folded his arms across his chest. Tarryall's peacemaker was a towering man in his forties who radiated power. He was by nature testy, brusque, highly capable and challenging – qualities he'd brought with him when he was hired to clean up this town several years earlier. He'd done his job well. Serious crime was a thing of the past in Tarryall, and he had a brutally efficient record against the rustlers of the region, with the puzzling exception of the High T, and more recently, the tiny, struggling Lazy Y. Apart from these reputation-damaging blemishes Kindersley enforced the law rigorously through the court and his deputies, and was ever ready to back up both with fists or guns any time it proved necessary.

The high-flyers loved their sheriff but he had few friends on the poor side of town, nor in the middle strata where Tessa Dorling lived. The feeling was mutual.

'You don't fool me, Miss Britches,' he snapped, revealing his bias against women who refused to fit a certain mould. His voice was rough edged. 'This isn't about a handful of skinny-ribbed cows here, and both of us know it. You've been out to bring me down ever since your brother got killed and I went after your boyfriend for his murder—'

'Cole Gannon was not my boyfriend—'

'Your lousy, half-smart boyfriend who your kid brother caught raiding High T, and got his brains blown out for his trouble. So I went after him, and you never forgave me for it.' Kindersley gestured violently. 'This hogswill about losing more cows is just that in my opinion. Hogswill! You'd hatch up any damned lie in order to make me look bad. But you're dropping your bucket down a dry well there, madam. I am the law here, I'll always be the law and one day, maybe soon, I'll be county sheriff while you'll still be chasing broomtails and crowbait cows through the brush. County high sheriff, hear me? Not bad for an Ohio river boy who ate catfish three times a day, eh?'

Kindersley bit off his words abruptly, paling under his deep bronze. He'd gone farther than he wanted, felt he'd revealed something of himself he'd rather keep hidden.

Tessa made to speak but he wasn't listening.

'I'll send the deputies out when I can spare them,' he snapped, swinging away across the plank landing. 'If your beef was stolen, we'll find it. But if we find you're faking these stories you'll wind up behind bars, female or not, believe that if you never believed anything else, madam!'

The sheriff was riled but had regained his composure by the time he hit the street. He paused before one of the huge man-made caves to hitch at his gunbelt and glanced upwards. From a narrow office window a handsome blonde woman was watching him, just as he anticipated. He saluted and she waved in reply. Mrs Slater Whitney was visiting town today to prepare their town mansion for the family's regular winter sojourn. Her husband wouldn't be in until the first snow; he was far too busy out on High T trying to cope with the rustlings which allegedly had brought him to the brink of ruin.

The face disappeared.

Kindersley straightened his string tie and glanced back. The Dorling woman was still where he'd left her, staring after him speculatively, but hopefully looking just a little less sure of herself now; it was hard to be certain with that one.

His lip curled. 'Spiteful damn spinster,' he muttered, then set off along the street, his familiar vigorous stride marred only slightly by the limp he carried as a legacy of a gun battle on the plains a year earlier. Arms swinging freely, head tilted slightly to one side and the star on his chest dull in the thin light, this was the law of Tarryall and looked it every inch.

The sheriff rarely rode or drove about in his flash buggy within the city limits. He believed in putting himself and the badge on show for the benefit of both the honest folk and the other kind at every opportunity. On the street, on foot and on duty twenty-four hours a day. That was the Kindersley style and he wouldn't change it for any reason, much less some flibbertigibbet female range boss who had too much to say and far too high an opinion of herself in his book.

But the sheriff was a rational man. He knew damn well that his outburst at the depot had little to do with Tessa Dorling or her petty vendetta and everything to do with the burdens he carried these days.

This man who thought big and acted accordingly, saw his life as an ongoing chess game over which he was master. And mostly this was the case. It was only quite recently that Boyd Kindersley had grown aware of the threat of another and highly dangerous player in the big game, one who might conceivably pose a threat to his ultimate victory, even to his very survival. Unless, of course, he played his way out of trouble as adroitly and successfully as he'd always done in the past.

In chess, life, or on the streets, his natural mode of defence was attack. Today, despite his outwardly relaxed demeanor as he came off the bridge and made his way towards the Boar's Head, he was in full attack mode.

The whiskey was always excellent at the saloon. Leaning on the mahogany, Kindersley rinsed the smooth rye through his mouth, finally swallowed it. Another shot suggested itself but he passed up on it and was making for the louvred doors when he sighted the 'prospectors' from Lake Navajo.

He propped. Hardy and Birch were newcomers with a miners' licence who curiously spent most all of their time loafing around the streets. His streets. He'd come to suspect strongly that the pair nosed around too much and asked far too many questions to be legitimate. In truth, they preoccupied him so much that he'd run several checks on them which had failed to either confirm or deny their claim to be Cousin Jack miners. Right now he was feeling more certain than ever that they didn't ring true. And that disturbed him. He always liked to know who his friends or enemies were in order that he might deal with them accordingly.

Through personal observation, but mainly through reports on the two men from both his deputies and his small army of sycophants, the sheriff had become aware, disturbingly so, that Hardy and Birch displayed an unwonted interest in the turbulent events of a year ago involving a rustling, a killing and the pursuit of and the eventual escape by Tarryall's most wanted man, one Cole Gannon.

For reasons few could even begin to guess at, the sheriff viewed long-gone Gannon as the wild piece on his chessboard with the potential power to destroy his king. Seated at a table beneath a window, Hardy and Birch nodded in his direction as he went outside. The batwing doors swung though their arcs and came to a rest behind him as he stroked his heavy jaw, reflecting that this just seemed to be a day designed to test him out on all fronts. So, he could handle it. But maybe it was time to take a chat with an old acquaintance.

He might well regard the judge as a drunken old buffoon, but couldn't deny they were interdependent. A sober Murdoch could often provide the reassurance the sheriff seemed to need more and more these uncertain days.

A drape screening a side window of the Boar's

Head flicked as he started off. Those nosy 'miners' were watching him. Squaring his shoulders Kindersley immediately set off for the courthouse complex, making his undeviating way down the dead center of the street, giving way for nobody on horseback, wheels or boot leather.

Traffic opened up for him and stayed that way.

This was a Kindersley technique developed during his early days as peacemaker. It was a deliberate tactic to demonstrate to all that the man behind the badge was *numero uno,* and could walk how, when and wherever he pleased. Should the day ever come when he lacked the power and presence to get away with such a high-handed tactic, both sheriff and town would know he was through. Nobody was making book this day would come soon, if ever.

He located the judge, not in chambers but in his gloomy little cubby-hole of a windowless office cum retreat out in back by the clerks' offices. Murdoch, in shirtsleeves, string tie, black vest and striped pants had his black boots up on a scarred old desk and nursed a tumbler full of whiskey in the dim light.

'Sheriff,' he murmured calmly, revealing by his manner and resonant delivery just how much he'd taken aboard. Up to five or six fingers of booze, he might still react guiltily if caught out. Beyond that point however, the Lord High Chief Justice of the Supreme Court could wander in and Murdoch, primed on Dutch courage, might invite him to loosen his suspenders and join him. Bushy black eyebrows lifted enquiringly. 'What can I do for you?'

'That's an interesting question, Judge.'

'We live in interesting times, Sheriff.'

They were fencing. Despite the judge's fondness for strong liquor and a tendency, when drinking, to talk down to the sheriff, Kindersley was generally obliged to treat the man as an equal both socially and in their overlapping involvement with the law. Of course he regarded Murdoch as a weakling, yet one with a keen mind, acid tongue and a native shrewdness which you underestimated at your peril. But whether drunk or sober, presiding from the bench or consorting with bums and fallen doves on some back street, Murdoch had his finger on the pulse of Tarryall and that was a talent upon which this ambitious, driven lawman was frequently forced to draw.

He said, 'That Dorling woman was in again. Another rustling, or so she claims.'

'I know. Nice legs, eh?'

Standing before the desk, hands on hips and shell belt gleaming, Kindersley let that one go by him.

'Then I'll tell you something you don't know. I just saw those two at the Boar's Head. Again.'

'Which two would that be, Sheriff?'

Kindersley glared in venomous silence. Seemed he was dead right about the kind of a day this was. Directly or indirectly everyone and his brother seemed out to raise his hackles.

On the other end of this narrow-eyed look, the judge sat blinking through the gloom that was a permanent feature of this room, his wasted face darker, more gaunt and darkly cross-hatched with red veins than ever beneath bristling black eyebrows, and bulging forehead. His right cheek boasted a large mole or wart, his body within the black suit of clothing was slumped against the old pine table that served as his desk. Apart from bottle and glass the only other item on the table was a weighty book some two inches thick and well thumbed from constant use.

He rested his elbow on the book for support as he continued to meet the other's glare. Until Kindersley stepped back, irritated that he was being forced to speak first.

'Those bogus miners, Hardy and Birch. As if you didn't know.'

'Oh, them.' Murdoch leaned back in his chair, affecting nonchalance. 'Well, I've also made enquiries, as you suggested, but so far nothing meaningful on your, ah, suspects.'

'They're no dirt-digging miners, that much is certain. I had a deputy ride out to their lease Monday. They haven't turned a sod, yet they've been here three weeks.'

'Why don't you apprise me exactly who or what you suspect these individuals could be, Sheriff? That might expedite my enquiries significantly.'

'Undercovers.'

The judge blinked. 'Explain?'

Kindersley began pacing to and fro, looking anything but his customary assured self now. His forehead was filmed with sweat and he kcpt glancing at the door as he talked. It was not the subject under discussion that was affecting him. It was to do with this room, which he rarely visited.

'They're always watching me. They're asking questions all over town and have even buttonholed my deputies. This may sound outlandish to you, but I've a hunch that enemies out to undermine my position could have hired them to secure evidence against me in whatever underhanded, quasi-legal stinking way they might.' He halted. 'There, I've levelled with you at long last. Does that satisfy you, damnit?'

Murdoch calmly lifted his glass to his lips. He enjoyed the rare situation of being calm and easy while the other was agitated. It was almost always the other way round.

'Tell me, Sheriff, are there any significant areas of your many activities upon which you might prove vulnerable to the covert stratagems and machinations of, shall we say, crypto-investigative operations?'

'What?'

'Are you guilty of anything unlawful?'

'What the hell sort of a question is that? I'm the goddamn law.'

'Correction, sir.' The judge dropped a gnarled hand upon the book. 'The *Revised Statutes of New Mexico Territory 1865*, as you well know. This is the law, and you, Sheriff Kindersley, are merely the lawman. Therein lies a chasm of distinction. This book is without error but we men are not. Nor are we without sin.'

Kindersley drew closer. 'Are you hinting at something, old man? If you are, out with it.'

'Very well. Tarryall has never been more rife with gossip and rumor highly critical of you. The unsolved rustlings . . . going back to the Gannon affair . . . any number of things.'

'But you have one particular matter in mind, don't you? So, out with it.'

At last Murdoch showed unease. But he had just enough bottled courage on board to keep on.

'I'd most solemnly and respectfully suggest that you keep away from Slater Whitney's wife, Sheriff.'

Kindersley's backhanded slap swept Murdoch's crossed legs off the desk and almost tumbled him out of his chair. The flying bottle struck the wall and smashed, leaving a spreading stain.

'Why you righteous old hypocrite!' he hissed. 'That's just another dirty rumour without basis, and you know it.'

Murdoch was badly shaken but refused to resile. Hair dishevelled, twisted awkwardly in his chair, he wagged an admonitory finger.

'It is not rumor, Sheriff. I may have found nothing on your two miners, but I know for a fact that something is going on between you and Stella Whitney. It's my considered opinion you desire that woman. Just as you desire land and wealth and acclaim in public places. You want, Mr Kindersley. And that is your failing. You want too much. No matter what you get, you still crave more.'

Scorn rode the sheriff's mouth.

'Listen to you. You charge me with wanting too much when all you want is a bottle of rotgut and a corner to sleep it off in.' He gestured. 'A rat-hole like this. You poor, pathetic old ruin.'

It had never gone this far between them. They were interdependent. But this was knock-down and dragout, and Judge Murdoch was salvaging some half-forgotten pride and courage from his younger years.

'It's this room, isn't it, Sheriff?' he said with a look

of malicious cunning, half rising. 'It's not really Hardy and Birch or the Whitney woman that's your problem. This room throws you every time, doesn't it.' He spread his arms. 'See, no window. Just a pokey little doorway, and full of shadows . . . just imagine what it's like in here in the middle of a black night without one glimmer of light and— What, leaving already, Sheriff?'

Nobody ever won a one-on-one with Boyd Kindersley. Up until now, that was. He was gone with a curse, leaving a suddenly exhausted Murdoch to slump back into his chair, his expression a mixture of shame, triumph and tremulous uncertainty.

Maybe he'd gone too far?

Slowly and laboriously he opened the drawer in which he kept the *Revised Statutes of New Mexico Territory 1865*, his Bible. He put the book away and felt about for a moment before producing another bottle. A full one.

For the judge, there was always another bottle.

3
.45 Howdy

At the 9,000 feet level the air cut like an Apache scalp-axe.

Cole Gannon drew rein in the lee of a granite bluff which shielded him from the worst of the driving rain that had lashed the mountains all morning. The buckskin hung its head in bleak submission to the elements but the sturdy grulla stood impassively at the end of the lead rope, its only concession to the weather to swing its hindquarters to the wind.

This lofted ridgeline rearing out of the pine forests like some primitive leviathan of the divide, was far above the timber leases, the well-used trails and the sweeping rangelands of the Nacimientos which were Gannon's destination. Having cut west into the mountains proper many miles south of Tarryall the previous morning, he'd purposely taken the old silver trail up through the Huffaker Heights to link up with the Pawnee Trail, which he'd then followed as far as Stranger's Mountain before cutting back eastwards directly down towards Fall River County.

Stranger's Mountain lay just ten miles westward and high above Whetstone Ranch, his home for four years before he was driven out.

There was no valid reason to suggest he could be at any immediate risk here, returning stealthily and unannounced as he was, but not even a year on the dodge with a murder charge hanging over his head could change Gannon's nature. He'd never been reckless or given to taking fool risks. These characteristics had sustained him for thirty years and had been a feature of his success in carving a paying cow ranch out of the wilds up here. He was the quiet man whose judgement you could count on, and today that judgement backed up by trail savvy and gut instinct combined to ensure he took every care.

Thus far at least, prudence had paid off. From this bluff he could have been overlooking Big Pine Plateau, Mesa Verde and the Keylock Hills ranches – but for the rain. But he was in home territory. He'd made the full journey up without encountering trouble. And here, if your name happened to be Gannon and you spoke of trouble, you meant Kindersley trouble.

There was a temptation now to take the Big Pine trail fork that led down to the Whetstone just to see how the old place looked, one year on.

But it wasn't nostalgia or anything close that had drawn him back, so instead he followed a faint animal pad north-east for a mile or two before cutting down into a rugged valley. Beyond the valley, some five miles distant and 1,500 feet lower, lay Monument Rocks which landmarked the border between the mighty High T and the Dorlings' Lazy Y.

The grulla whickered. It remembered. The buckskin plodded on impassively as stone gave way to loamy soil beneath heavy hooves and the valley opened up before them.

It was a magical, timeless place despite the blurring rain that seemed to have a breath of snow in it. This was many miles beyond the plains where iron peaks thrust up on either side, thinning out and changing color as they became naked fingers of stone above the timber line.

The good earth was soft from all the rain and the horses plowed up the sod and raised a sweet, rich smell that was a million years old. He sure was back home.

Hunching shoulders beneath his mackinaw, Cole Gannon thought about his snug cabin, boiling hot coffee and that old buffalo robe he'd had to leave behind when he fled the county with a posse in hot pursuit.

He wanted a smoke so bad he ached for it. But he didn't stop, didn't start feeling his tobacco sack. Instead he focused on Tessa Dorling and her letters. Two rustling raids on the Lazy Y within weeks, and she plainly feared more to come since the law office in Tarryall had failed to make even a token attempt to investigate the crimes.

Of course there'd been no suggestion in the letters that Gannon could do anything about this crisis. In every letter she'd written regularly over the year she'd urged him to remain incognito in the south, warning that even if others might have forgotten him and his alleged crime, Boyd Kindersley certainly had not.

Down south he'd been just another drifting loner. Here he was branded killer and fugitive from justice.

Yet he'd provisioned up and journeyed 500 miles back to danger territory to help out without a second thought. Just as readily Tessa had once spent two weeks with him out along the Pecos nursing him back to health following the almost fatal showdown with the possemen at Arroyo.

It was the least a man could do. And with luck and a steady nerve he might get to do it successfully without winding up on a gallows.

Mid afternoon found him warily circling through the white pines and coarse undergrowth of the slopes which cupped the Lazy Y on its northern flank.

The rain had eased off some and it was bitter cold with a metallic curtain of mist drifting obliquely across the gloomy afternoon, and underfoot the going was growing even heavier from this rain and those before.

Eventually he stashed the horses in a sheltered draw, slipped the carbine from its scabbard and continued on through the dripping woods until gaining a high grassy hummock overlooking a meadow.

Directly across this meadow lay a narrow canyon and above the gradually rising benchland beyond stood the familiar acres of Lazy Y.

It was good to see the ranch once more. But no time for memories of good times, easy friendships, red violence and tragedy right now. Rustler trouble had brought him back, and the tranquil appearance of the ranch didn't fool him for a moment.

Only now did he hunker down in back of the hummock to shape the Durham he badly needed. The brief flare of the match tinted the taut and watchful features of a hunter. The fugitive wanted to believe he was the same man who'd lived here before, but inside was all too aware of the change, the hardness and hickory toughness that hadn't been part of his make-up before the sheriff of Tarryall tried to frame him for murdering a friend.

Gene Dorling, just twenty-three and full of life had been that friend. Tessa's kid brother.

With infinite patience he studied the wide landscape.

Confronted with any problem or challenge, he liked to examine it from all angles, keep his own counsel then rely on his own decisions. A survivor's code.

What he quickly decided here was that something about the Lazy Y simply didn't sit right. It took him a long patient time to figure what it was. Down along the south graze where the timber crowded the boundary fence stood a stand of heavy oaks on the ranch side. Perfect shelter from cold, drizzling rain. Yet several hundred yards distant he could see cattle hunched miserably beneath a scatter of leaking cottonwoods.

How come?

Seemed there could be no good reason for a critter to forsake good shelter for poor unless something had spooked it away.

This led him to focus attention exclusively upon

the timberline close by the oaks. Visibility was poor with the daylight slowly fading, and it wasn't until he drew his battered old Army issue field-glasses from beneath his slicker and began panning the timber that he struck pay dirt.

At first sighting he imagined the wisp of movement against the dark of the trunks to be simply a finger of rain or mist. But when the sighting was repeated some time later, he fixed his glasses on the specific spot for maybe a minute before emitting a short grunt of satisfaction.

The brownish object amongst the brush he'd been focusing on suddenly took the shape of a man's hat. He then made out the paler oval of a face beneath, followed by another wisp of gray curling through the air.

The hidden man was smoking.

Lazy Y was staked out!

Slowly Gannon lowered the glasses and sat Indian-still for the time it took to roll and smoke a second quirley. His eyes were bleak and cold. Not for a moment did he believe other than that whatever was going on down there, whoever it might be keeping furtive surveillance over Tessa's house, it had to add up as some kind of danger for her and old Perce.

That was all he needed to know.

Slithering away from the hummock, he back-tracked to the treeline then followed it downwards.

It was almost dark when he reached the elms where the man had been hiding. He wasn't there any longer. But scouting around he found not one but two sets of boot tracks in the wet grass, which he followed through to the fence where the men had clambered over to head upslope towards the ranch house on foot.

His Colt was in his fist as he vaulted the fence. He was thinking rustlers, but it could be anyone. Anyone with evil intent, that was. Honest men didn't act this way.

He reached the tumbledown hay barn without incident. Lights glowed warmly from the house a hundred yards distant. The intervening space was broken by a corral, two outbuildings, a wagon shed and the wellhouse, all in advanced stages of decay.

Otherwise everything appeared normal as blueberry pie but for the twin sets of distinct footprints leading away from his corner towards the dark bulk of the wagon shed.

He waited.

It was maybe a minute before he heard the faint brush of leather against timber. This was followed by a soft curse, a murmur of voices. His men were sheltering beneath the dripping eaves of the shed on the dark side away from the light, and eventually, by slitting his eyes and concentrating, he found he could make out the dim silhouettes.

Seemed a damnfool curious way for cattle thieves to be acting – if that's what they were.

Suddenly, the pair detached themselves from the black shape of the shed and headed back his way. One tallish and the other short and blocky, both wore weather gear and carried revolvers in their hands.

Gannon had a handful of seconds to reach a decision. The men halted abruptly at the sound of the tiny, lethal triple click of his Colt hammer being thumbed back.

His voice knifed out at them from the darkness. 'Shuck those guns and reach. This is the law!'

He had no way of knowing his words were a dead giveaway for a brace of badgepackers. Cursing, leaping apart, they jerked up their weapons and the misting quiet of the Lazy Y evening was ripped apart by the churn of gunfire, billowing flares of Colt flame chewing holes out of the darkness.

Going low, Gannon triggered back, deliberately keeping his aim low. 'Don't be loco!' he shouted above the uproar. 'I've got you outlined, you fools!'

The response he drew as the pair rushed for the opposite end of the barn, hit him like a bullet. 'It's Gannon! It's gotta be!'

They knew! But how was that possible? Nobody knew!

A sharp breath of hot air whipped past his face as a gun cracked venomously. He was instantly upright and streaking along the darkened flank of the shed, six-gun at the ready, taking the battle to the enemy before they could recover from their shock.

The two men were cursing and stumbling over one another by the doors beneath the weather awning as he lunged into sight round the clapboard corner. Giving them no time to react, he attacked panther-quick to crunch gunbarrel against a hard head, sending the squat figure thudding to the ground with blood gushing from his ear.

His companion triggered wildly and Gannon went low, firing upwards blindly. There was a howl of pain, an explosive curse and next moment he was alone on the grass with the motionless figure of the first man sprawled at his side, legs and arms akimbo, houselight dim upon the brass star on his barrel chest.

Law!

Gannon was too confounded even to cuss. He was on his feet and round the corner in jig time, but the lanky figure of the second man was already well clear of the building and chewing up distance in leaping strides on the downhill slope as he made for the fence.

Gannon's gun kicked back against the base of his thumb as he laid a shot deliberately above the bobbing head. The running figure ducked but seemed to find added reserves of speed as the darkness swallowed him.

Breathing hard, Gannon lowered the smoking gun, only now growing aware of the clamor coming from the house, the frenzied barking of the dog, the banging of a door, voices calling in confusion.

He spun round to see a familiar slim figure toting a rifle on the back porch with a blockier shape filling the kitchen window to Tessa Dorling's left.

'Who is it?' she cried, and despite the uncertainty of the situation he realized she sounded anything but afraid. 'Come on, show yourself or I'll—'

'Don't shoot, Tessa!' he shouted. 'It's me, Cole.'

'Cole?'

'Well that clinches it for good and all,' Perce Dorling rumbled from the depths of his great old chair, which like himself had seen far better times. 'Three rustlin' raids, no help from the law, now goldurn Kindersley deppities stakin' out our place and tryin' to murder Cole just like they done to my boy! A man's gotta know when he's had enough. We're sellin' up, daughter woman. That's final.'

'We're not selling.'

Coming from the kitchen where she was fixing coffee and sandwiches, Tessa's voice was calm, firm and just a tad weary; the repetitive tone of a mother dealing with a troublesome child.

'We're sellin' up. We'll end up all gettin' murdered in our beds, goddamnit. They could've killed us tonight and only for the boy they would've, most likely.'

The old man tossed his head fretfully. He'd never been the same since a fall from his horse some years earlier, while the death of his son the previous year had sent him spiralling into decline. He continued complaining and banging his hand down on the armrest until Tessa came through with a plate of sandwiches and a steaming pannikin of coffee. Then he was quiet, leaving her free to return to the back to stare off into the darkness where Gannon had vanished in search of the second man.

She didn't relax until she saw his tall figure emerge from the shed with a coil of rope over one shoulder, and just the sight of him seemed as calming and reassuring as she remembered. She remembered other things about him also, like the clean smell of the outdoors that seemed to surround him; the sound of his voice, as calming as sun-warmed water running over river stones.

'No sign!' he called. 'I found one horse and set it loose. Duggan took off on the other. I've got the fat one trussed and gagged in the shed. You can set him loose later . . . and you folks will know nothing, Tessa. Understand?'

She nodded and stepped aside for him, holding the screen door open.

Gannon's return had already been tainted by violence. But Tessa had regained her full composure as he sat to table in the kitchen and she placed the food and coffee before him then stood back to watch him eat. He glanced at her, reflecting on her wild, welcoming hugs and the initial excitement of their reunion, so unlike this formidable young woman. Now she had returned to her disciplined self, but the feeling remained good between them. They'd shared so much.

'I still can't believe you're back, Cole. But you shouldn't be. You realize that, don't you?'

Gannon munched a cold beef and cornbread sandwich. He'd forgotten he hadn't eaten since dawn, somewhere out along the Pawnee Trail. He was ravenous and relieved, doubly relieved that he hadn't had to kill anybody. That was not why he'd come back.

'It sure enough crossed my mind when the gunplay started, Tess,' he conceded. He frowned at the windows. 'They were expecting me, you know? Waiting for me. They knew just who I was out there even in the rain and the dark. But how, do you figure? You didn't even know I was heading back, no one did. But those two deputies were watching out for me. And their sign I found down there in the trees says they've been lurking around for days in the brush, maybe longer—'

'The letters!' she cut in abruptly, startling him.

She clapped her hands to her lips, a familiar gesture. 'Oh, Cole, I've been trying and trying to figure how on earth Kindersley could have guessed you might show up, and it only just struck me. It has to be my letters to you telling you about our rustling troubles. Good Lord! I should have anticipated how you'd react to that news. Kindersley plainly did.'

'Hey, steady, you're not making sense, girl. Nobody ever saw those letters but you and me.'

But Tessa had the bit between her teeth, her whole face animated as she spoke fast.

'Boyd Kindersley can find out just about anything he wants in Tarryall. We should both know that. And it just struck me that one of his drinking buddies at the Deacon's Bench is the postmaster.' Her eyes widened. 'Cole, don't you see how it could have been done? Had Kindersley wanted to find out if we were communicating – if he'd wanted access to my letters. Do you think that weak-kneed postmaster would deny him access to my letters? Would he dare?'

Gannon's appetite was gone. He stared up at her in silence, one objection jostling with another in his mind. Yet surely what she was saying made solid sense, he had to admit. Somehow, some way, Boyd Kindersley had to have known he would show up here.

'The whole thing is pure Kindersley,' Tess said intensely, no longer merely surmising now; convinced. She enumerated on her fingers. 'I lose some worthless cattle to rustlers. I write you. Kindersley makes no attempt to deal with the rustling, because of course it's his doing. You and I both know he's a cow thief, and far worse. And the man is so clever, Cole. He would figure, that if it were humanly possible, you would respond by coming back here to help out. So – so then he planted his deputies here and had them lying in wait to murder you when you did. My stars, it's so plain, so terrifyingly obvious. Surely you can see it?'

Gannon rose and toted his coffee out to the back porch. The rain had ceased but the roof was leaking. Lazy Y headquarters, never flash, had gone to hell in a handbasket over the space of a year without a man around to handle the heavy chores.

He rested elbows on the rickety railing, his thoughts racing now.

Kindersley was capable of anything, he had to agree. Last year's murderous incident in which Gannon and Gene Dorling had surprised Kindersley, his ranch ramrod and hands in the act of rustling prime beef down from the High T, and the subsequent shooting of Gene and the framing of him for the crime, was incontestable proof of this. And he supposed he had to agree at least with the possibility that the big man was quite capable of securing access to Tessa's mail. Once having established that the two friends were maintaining regular contact, all that remained for the sheriff was to mount a couple of token raids on the Lazy Y then sit back and wait for 'hero' Gannon to swallow the bait and come riding back like a knight errant, hopefully to get himself killed.

And he'd almost blundered into the trap!

He turned to stare at Tessa in silence and she could see their thoughts were now running in tandem.

'That bastard!' he said softly. Then he shook his head. 'But it all adds up, Tess. For even when Kindersley found out you were writing me down south, he knew there'd be no way he could round me up there. But plainly he was desperate to get me back, and nobody ever said that man is a fool. So he put on his thinking cap. Lay the right bait, then haul me in like a goddamn catfish. And I of course swallowed it down whole.'

'Only you would do a thing like that, Cole.'

She spoke warmly but he wasn't listening. He was now a bloodhound on the scent of something big. Kindersley big. He nodded slowly. 'So, okay. Now we reckon we know how and what he did, but it doesn't explain why.'

'Perhaps it does.'

'Huh?'

Tessa moved to join him at the railing, the wind stirring her raven curls. A deathly cold held the rangeland in its grip tonight. Snow cold.

'I visited with Kindersley just this week. He was his usual arrogant self, patronizing and overbearing. But now I recall he appeared very tense underneath, and apparently he's been upsetting even his admirers in town recently with his temper and caustic tongue. I believe he's even had brushes with Slater Whitney, and not even the sheriff can afford that.'

'Interesting. But what's it add up to, girl?'

Tessa met his eyes levelly. 'The signs all point to Kindersley being under heavy pressure, Cole. Don't you think it's possible, considering the crazy lengths it appears he's gone to to trap you, that you might be the cause of this strain.'

This seemed to make sense, but only up to a point. 'But how the hell could I be that important, Tess? Racked up against the big fish Kindersley mingles with, Cole Gannon's just a minnow.'

'Perhaps only time will tell.' Tessa's manner now turned brisk. 'In the meantime, he'll show up here soon enough now. So we had better decide on how best to keep you safe and alive, hadn't we.'

'Curious thing, Tess, but standing here right now looking over the spread, and despite everything that's happened, I've never felt I wanted to stay alive more.'

'That's because you're back home, Cole.'

Home. Good word. Dangerous in his case, no doubt. But it sounded real fine even so.

4
He's Back!

'Sure it was Gannon,' slurred the blocky deputy, tenderly fingering his gashed temple. The man stared accusingly at Tessa Dorling, standing with arms folded by the open fire. 'Her old buddy, so it was. He was lyin' in wait for us out by the shed, tried to kill us so he did. You bring Bob in and he'll confirm what I'm sayin'.'

'Nobody else is entering this house, Deputy,' Tessa said coldly. 'And now that you have some notion of what happened here, Sheriff, you may leave.'

Kindersley's eyes flared from across the room but he remained controlled. Outside, shivering in the night wind, were the two deputies and the ramrod from his small ranch who'd accompanied him out to Lazy Y following the deputy's return to town with news of the Gannon incident. Gannon. The sheriff had offered no explanation as to why the Y had been under surveillance, while in response the Dorlings claimed no knowledge of who'd been involved in the shoot-out with his men.

It was a stand-off.

Kindersley was mad clear through; you could feel his suppressed fury like heat coming off a branding iron. He'd had two deputies worked over, his secret surveillance of the spread revealed, was now confronted yet again by a woman he both detested and suspected. But he'd gone as far as he dared tonight with Tessa Dorling, who for some reason beyond his understanding seemed to be the darling of all the small ranchers and other members of the county's anti-Kindersley faction. Some even went so far as to label her attractive.

They had to be kidding. The sheriff liked women who looked and acted like women.

'You haven't heard the last of this, Miss Britches,' he said softly, snatching his Stetson down from the elkhorn rack. 'This is not the first time I've had reason to suspect you of aiding and abetting a wanted murderer, the same low-life in fact who killed your own brother—'

'Cole Gannon did not kill Gene,' she cut him off. 'We both of us know exactly who did, and I'd bear that in mind if I were you, Sheriff Kindersley.'

With a curt gesture to his battered deputy, Kindersley reefed the door open and strode out on to the muddied porch.

The man named Strummer stirred so sharply his heavy rowel spurs jingled. The sheriff's ramrod was somewhere in his mid-thirties, tall, bobcat lean, wearing yellow roper's gloves and a blanket coat with buckskin patches on the elbows.

'Ain't we takin' the dame in, boss?' the man puzzled as the sheriff strode for the horses standing miserably at the tie rack.

'Get mounted, damn you!' was Kindersley's brusque response. 'All of you, goddamnit!' Filling his saddle, he shot a parting glare at the slim figure framed in the lighted doorway. 'We've got a killer to track down, remember! Let's go.'

They followed his tall figure from the ranchyard, the deputies' hurricane lamps bobbing as they receded swiftly in the direction of the main gate and the town trail. The door slammed defiantly hard behind them but Boyd Kindersley didn't look back. Already he was scanning the wet ground for sign of the fugitive but there was none to be found. Cole Gannon had vanished. Again.

'He's back! Cole Gannon's back from the grave!'

This was the cry that jolted Tarryall awake next morning before first light, immediately touching off an excited reaction and reigniting the fire under an old and prickly debate. Namely, was the former Stranger's Mountain cowman and well-liked man about Tarryall guilty of the murder of young Gene Dorling? Or was he, as many had never stopped contending, the victim of a gross error and almost criminal mishandling of that entire affair on the part of their sheriff?

Tarryall might never know the truth of that incident which had taken place during one of the earliest and biggest rustling raids against the High T. Yet it seemed that by first light today 'most everybody had a pretty clear idea of what had taken place out at the Lazy Y just on darkdown last night. Namely, that two deputies had been surveying the Dorling spread – nobody seemed to know why – and Gannon had shown up out of no place to trade shots with the pair, creasing one and putting him to flight and leaving the other trussed up like a Thanksgiving turkey.

Threatening to revive the whole controversy of the Gannon–Kindersley saga as it did, and with the whole town agog to the startling news, it was small wonder that the new day seemed well under way before Tarryall belatedly realized the county had changed color overnight.

The snow had come silently and stealthily in the deep of the night and this morning the Sangre de Cristo lay under a blanket of white.

In no time the bundled up children were out playing noisily in the street, and even the heady news about Gannon was quickly relegated to second place. Sure, the topic would continue to enliven bar room debate and street corner gossip, but the first snow and what it meant here would surely dominate, at least for the day.

The old-timers and self-styled weather experts might claim that this snow was not the real thing; they liked to see winter kick off with a howling blizzard, but that didn't signify. Traditionally the first fall of any kind of snow was regarded as the official start of the winter which was widely regarded as the better part of the year in Fall River County.

There was a limit to how much meaningful work could take place in mines, at timber leases or on the ranches once the snow season arrived, and with country people tending to come to town far more at this time of year, diverting and entertaining events were already being planned with socializing and good times looming as a welcome relief from hard work and isolation.

By mid-morning the good ladies of the Tarryall Christian Women's Association, managing to successfully ignore all the comings and goings at the law office and the ongoing hubbub relating to the Gannon affair, were already locked into a major meeting at the church hall to undertake some serious forward planning. Their purpose, as always this time of year, was to ensure that their town enjoyed an uplifting, peaceful and productive wintertide – before the menfolk could get to wreck it all with their gambling, drinking and even worse.

The same worthy ladies deemed it the best of all possible portents for a great season when the muted sounds of hooves and rubber-tyred wheels crossing the big bridge drew them to the clubhouse's frosted windows to see the handsome coach and four coming in from the direction of the High T. The Whitneys' arrival to take up residence in their town mansion on Catamount Street was traditionally viewed as signalling the official onset of the social season. And surely today, in light of last night's disturbing events, having Mr Whitney on hand would be doubly welcome.

Slater Whitney, they reminded one another as the heavy rosewood Concord came sweeping grandly by, was not only the region's most esteemed citizen by far, but was and had always been its social icon. His ideals were of the very highest while his spheres of commercial and political influence reached all the way to the halls of power at the County Capital and beyond; some said as far as Washington itself.

Tarryall relied upon 'the Colonel' and his glamorous wife to give focus and dignity to the social season, and hoped their arrival might divert attention from last night's disturbance.

For it was regarded in Tarryall, even here in the inner, conservative circle of Republican supporters of the current Sheriff Kindersley–Judge Murdoch-led administration, that their esteemed sheriff, whose once-high popularity had been significantly slipping for a year and more now, didn't seem to be handling this latest crisis all that well. Worst of all, much as they might like to sweep it under the carpet, the mothers of Tarryall were fully aware that Gannon's comeback would revive all the bitter rancour, disagreement and suspicion associated with the Dorling killing and its aftermath – the bloody posse-versus-Gannon showdown in the desert.

Thank the good Lord Mr Whitney had arrived right on cue to spread his calming influence. And to show him exactly how they felt the ladies flung the clubhouse windows wide to wave lace kerchiefs as the handsomest equipage in the mountains swept grandly by.

'Anyone got any chicken feed?' smirked the slim young man with brushed-back hair seated within the coach. He waved mockingly at the crowded windows. 'C'mon, you old hens, feeding time.'

'Lonnie, stop that!'

The woman seated opposite the Whitneys' son and heir was still on the sunny side of forty, blonde, buxomly attractive and only slightly overdressed in furs and furbelows topped off by a dramatic off the face tulle hat with wooden cherries ornamenting the sweeping brim.

'Chick, chick, chick!' her son said defiantly, and Stella Whitney turned appealingly to her husband seated by the far window.

'Slater!'

The tall and impeccably dressed man smiled tolerantly. Handsome and distinguished with a white streak through his dark hair, Slater Whitney was a man in his prime who could maintain dignity and bearing despite great adversity – in his case, the all but ruinous campaign of rustling attacks upon his giant spread. A social, political and commercial heavyweight, his breeding was reflected in his attire, that sculpted smile, the air of refinement he wore like a cloak. He nodded.

'Lonnie's right. They are a bunch of old hens.'

'There's no need for him to be rude, Slater.'

The boy crossed his legs and locked hands behind his head, his pale, good-looking face petulant now.

'You're not planning on nagging me all winter, are you, mother?'

'I don't nag,' she said. 'Slater, do I nag?'

'Well, perhaps sometimes it might sound to Lonnie as though you do, Stella,' came the diplomatic reply. Then Whitney leaned forward, gazing out. 'Hmm, there's Kindersley and some of his people. Looks somewhat tense today, wouldn't you agree, m'dear?'

The boy slid across the seat to peer out. They were passing the jailhouse with its roof heavy with snow. On the broad front porch, hatless and wearing a belted leather jacket, his thumbs hooked into the gunbelt, Boyd Kindersley was speaking with a deputy, the reporter from the *County Express*, and a whipcord-lean figure sporting a gaudy blanket jacket and tied down six-shooter.

The group didn't look up at the coach's approach; they were intent on what Kindersley was saying.

'Strange business this Gannon affair,' Whitney continued. 'I suppose I assumed as everyone did that he'd died as a result of that gunfight down in Arroyo last year. I'm rather gratified that we seem to have been proven wrong.' He frowned. 'But you'd wonder what on earth would bring the fellow back, considering the danger it places him in. I expect it will resurrect all the gossip that flared up around our sheriff at that time.' A pause. 'Don't you agree, Stella? All that nasty gossip about just what really did happen the night young Dorling was killed?'

'I'm sure it's no concern of mine what folks might want to say about Sheriff Kindersley, Slater.'

'Want to bet?' her son said slyly.

Stella flushed. 'And just what is that supposed to mean, Lonnie?'

The boy shrugged insolently and folded his arms. 'Nothing, I guess.' At just twenty years of age, Lonnie Whitney was spoiled, pampered and over-indulged by a doting father and was largely ignored by an anything but doting mother. Stella Whitney, who had married her husband early during his climb to wealth and power, had never really taken to motherhood, had scarcely distinguished herself as a wife either for that matter. She regarded her husband as aloof and snobbish, her son as a generally nasty little creation with a possibly unstable side to him, plus some genuinely unpleasant habits – such as a deep-rooted mistrust of herself that seemed highlighted by his adoration of his father.

But luckily there was an opposite and compensatory side to these ongoing concerns, and the woman was reminded vividly of just another of these as the rig swung into Catamount Street and made its slowing way through the slushy snow to turn in through the towering gates of the mansion. The Whitney ranch house out on High T was large and handsomely appointed, yet their town house almost put it to shame.

It was a good 500 feet of carefully trimmed lawns now hidden under white between the gates and the front gallery of the house, and twin rows of poplars lined the curved drive which had been shovelled clear in anticipation of their arrival. The gleaming windows and imposing white columns of possibly the grandest house in the county were the visible, tangible reassurances of just about everything that was important to Stella Whitney.

Almost, but not quite.

The woman allowed husband and son to alight and make their way for the house, arm in arm, before she too stepped down, a footman taking her elbow.

She swung sharply to gaze back towards Pawnee, hoping to catch another glimpse of Boyd Kindersley, but the sheriff was nowhere to be seen. Likely already out on the trails again beating the brush for Cole Gannon, she assumed. She sighed gustily. She couldn't care less about Gannon, who after all had gunned Kindersley down in Arroyo and might well have put him in his grave. She couldn't understand all this uproar about the man's return. It seemed as though now, as had been the case last year, so many people who should know better regarded Gannon as sinned against rather than sinning.

With a small cluck of annoyance, Stella flipped her beaver stole around one shoulder and followed her family inside where the servants were lined up to greet them. She hoped that Gannon would simply vanish again as he'd done before. She hoped to see more of the lawman now they'd come to town for the season, not less.

Cole Gannon powered the grulla through a snow-drift then reined in to stare back, realizing he was no longer alone on this lonesome stretch of the Pawnee Trail.

At what precise moment he'd come to this understanding was not clear. It was an instinctive thing. His instincts, always highly tuned then honed razor sharp during his exile on the Rio Hondo, had simply sensed something first, some small intrusive element in this still and gleaming snowscape, well before his eyes got to pick it up.

There was now something different about this familiar stretch of trail leading him towards Stranger's Mountain and his home basin. His senses kept crying it until, sure enough, he sighted what he was searching for moving across the open face of Mesa Verde off to the south-east, a single tiny speck of motion whose deliberate undeviating line assured him it wasn't a wild animal but a man on horseback.

Had to be trouble.

Whoever it was had either picked up his trail, or was just taking a punt that the fugitive might head back to his home acres in the wake of last night's dust-up.

His fingers were steady as he fashioned a smoke from tobacco and papers, licked the construction into a neat white cylinder then touched a match to it.

Of course he'd been on the lookout for something like this. Kindersley had attempted to kill him before, and obviously had every desperate reason for wanting him dead right now. For apart from the sheriff s henchmen, Cole Gannon was the only man living who knew how Gene Dorling had really met his death.

He'd been gunned down by Kindersley and Strummer as they rode with the pack of rustler scumdogs running stock off the High T.

That night a year ago, Gannon and Gene Dorling had been absent from the Lazy Y on a horse drive down to the Crockett Range. That proved to be the same night a pack of nightriders staged a major raid on Whitney's ranch and, as they had done before, ran the stock off by the swiftest and most convenient route, namely directly across the adjacent Lazy Y at stampede speed.

Only thing, Gannon and Dorling returned ahead of time after a Lazy Y messenger reached their drive with the news that Perce Dorling's health had taken a serious turn for the worse.

The two rode straight into hell with all the fences down – stampeding cattle raging across the spread in the moonlight lashed on by yipping riders with blazing guns.

They tried to intervene; any cowman would do the same. The brief and brutal shoot-out saw two rustlers and Gene Dorling dead in the dust with a wounded Gannon barely managing to escape with his life and a bunch of riders headed up by Boyd Kindersley in hot pursuit on what proved to be a sixty-mile journey which ended on the bloody streets of Arroyo twenty-four hours later.

He'd seen Strummer and Kindersley cut Gene down; would carry that vividly horrific picture in his memory forever.

Was it any wonder that the sheriff should want him dead and silenced? He'd lived for a year with the knowledge that the lawman who had driven the wild men out of Tarryall and set up a judicial system second to none in the region, was involved in large-scale rustling from High T compounded by murder and the swearing of false charges against himself. Kindersley was a criminal of the most sinister and dangerous breed; a corrupt peace officer. That was the chilling truth of what a then innocent Cole Gannon had unwittingly uncovered that night. 'And yet,' whispered the back of his mind even now as it had done so often over that long year, 'who would believe it?'

The speck was a blob by this time.

With a jerk of the reins Gannon cut the horse away from the drift and raced towards the timber-line. He rode with a sureness stemming from total familiarity with the terrain. There were things he needed from the Whetstone, essential things which he still planned to get regardless. He calculated he had ample time to get there, get what he wanted and get gone before that horseman got anywhere close.

This was war. But hadn't he expected precisely that when he made the decision to return? More importantly, did it signify? He was back. That was all that counted. He was all through running and hiding. He was glad he'd come now, the danger notwithstanding. He would see it through and see Kindersley have his day in court, or – what? Die? His jaw muscles clamped tight. Maybe so, Gannon. Death had to be always on the cards in a game like this. But if it came to that he would go down fighting. If nothing else he reckoned he'd prove desperately hard to kill, especially when he knew that his true enemy here was Tarryall's law.

The snowy woods swallowed him.

5

Trouble at Whetstone

In the back room of the Deacon's Bench Saloon, Sheriff Kindersley finished shaving by the soft glow of the lamp he'd had lighted, even though darkness was still an hour off. Leaning forward, he studied the reflection of his powerful face with its cap of rust-colored hair and cleft chin. He shrugged into the leathern jacket that had cost him thirty dollars, tailor-made, from Gruber and Sons, Kansas City. Off-the-rack stuff was invariably too tight in the shoulders for the sheriff of Tarryall.

He splashed a jolt of the saloonkeeper's private bourbon stock into a glass from a desk decanter, and rolled it round his mouth as he moved closer to the lamp and stared fixedly at the gentle flame. Then he raised the glass in a mocking salute to the picture of the President the saloonkeeper kept on the wall above his desk, and swallowed.

The early evening was just getting under way as he went out into the bar room. The saloonkeeper nodded and smiled from the poker layout where he sat with friends. Kindersley's nod was distant. He had free use of even the inner sanctum here and expected nothing less. As did many in Tarryall, the saloonman owed him plenty and knew the value of staying on good terms with him.

A piano began to tinkle and a woman laughed shrilly as he threaded his way between mostly empty tables. He shot a sharp glance in the direction of the sound but saw that the woman's group was not even aware of his presence. He was alert for any hint of derision or criticism in the aftermath of Gannon's return.

The gossips were having a field day.

The Kindersley chess board was growing crowded.

The case keeper, brooding from his high chair above the faro layout with a bottle within easy reach, gestured respectfully. Kindersley nodded back then stepped out through the doors to feel the bite of the cold against freshly shaven skin.

Two men were approaching and he gave them a sharp look. Just a couple of High T hands in town on a spree. Not Hardy and Birch, those so-called miners. On the sheriff's chess board, that pair and their ongoing presence in town continued to concern him for the solid reason that they still didn't ring true to him. He played for such high stakes that he must always know who and what he was up against, what player might be holding a full hand and who might be bluffing. With Hardy and Birch, he was anything but sure. Still.

He paused on the next corner to light a cheroot. The misting night was drawing on, muffling the familiar sounds of his town. From somewhere along

Coyote Street came the boisterous yip of a skylarking cowboy. A bulky figure in a poncho clomped past him with a muttered, 'Evenin', Shurf.'

There might be plenty loose talk but every man-Jack of them still knew who called the shots, he mused with satisfaction. And it wasn't some ragged-assed rancher-cum-outlaw on the run either. The lawman might not be as popular as he once was, but he was still the man who had tamed their town. He would continue to be *the* man on main street until he chose otherwise.

Hopefully that day would come when the High T was in his pocket the way Tarryall was now.

He crossed the street to encounter two twittering matrons from the Christian Society hurrying homewards late after a day spent gossiping and organizing the winter's social calendar.

'Oh, Sheriff Kindersley, how lovely to see you looking so calm and reassuring in the midst of all this awful gossip.'

And, 'All we ladies are one hundred per cent behind you, Sheriff. There is always envy and enmity directed towards great men, and that cap certainly fits you to a T. God bless and protect you. Your duties are so dangerous and you handle them so bravely and honourably. We're proud of you.'

'Thank you, ladies.'

It might be only a pair of housewives from the conservative side of town, he reflected as he continued on, but they were still representative of the important faction he'd won over so completely here – before the bug of ambition sank its fangs into prime hide and began to erode his popularity.

He'd remained contaminated ever since that day, but the 'infection' he lived with now only made him stronger and more focused than ever before in his turbulent life. That specific day had seen him stand, cap in hand before the full town council to hear its response to his request for a hefty pay increase and a contract of long tenure, only to receive a heavy-handed 'no' on both counts.

It still rankled.

With sudden clarity Boyd Kindersley had awoken to the realization that he was pushing forty-five with little to look back on but a murky past topped off by several years of genuine service behind the badge here. Until suddenly here he was with the future lurking round the corner offering little better than middle age and likely poverty.

By the time he quit the chambers that very day he was a changed man. He might still look the same, was still regarded as arrogant and at times overbearing and continued to keep the town every bit as clean and law-abiding as ever. But underneath nothing was the same. Like St Paul's enlightenment on the road to Damascus, the sheriff's transformation from committed peace officer to a ruthless man consumed by ambition was total and complete.

Now pay-off time was at hand. And the pay-off for all the work and sweat and hair-raising risks he had taken would surely become reality, the critics, hitches and the unforeseen notwithstanding.

Disguising his limp more effectively than ever, his stride reflected his confidence and offered no comfort to his detractors as he continued on to the law office and stepped beneath the thick arch of the doorway.

Within were two of his deputies, the newspaper editor leaning back in his chair clutching a bar of the cell door to balance himself, the turnkey standing by the pot belly fixing coffee and Judge Murdoch occupying Kindersley's chair at his desk and showing no inclination to vacate it.

Everyone began speaking at once. Kindersley had been unavailable all day. He still was. He wasn't here to mull over the incident at the Lazy Y which still had Tarryall standing on its ear, they quickly realized. He was here but briefly to hear reports on the manhunt and to issue orders. He did so with customary brisk efficiency, observed with brute apathy from the cells by the drunken miner he'd arrested the previous night, with violence. The prisoner's face was like raw steak. The sheriff played the game hard.

'Well, carry on,' he snapped as he made for the door. He waved the newsman aside and attempted to do the same to the judge, but somehow Murdoch beat him to the archway.

'We must talk, Sheriff,' he slurred *sotto voce.* 'It's essential you make some public statement to shore up your position in response to all the innuendo and suchlike that is sweeping over this town like an avalanche.'

'You give a statement. Talking is your forte.'

The ruined old face reddened.

'Damn you, Kindersley! Everybody wants to know why you had the Lazy Y staked out that way, don't you understand? Tessa Dorling has been spreading all kinds of insinuations around and—'

He broke off as Kindersley pressed something into his palm. It was a silver dollar. Kindersley patted the man's cheek where the wart stood out like a peg driven into the flesh.

'Buy yourself a fifth, Judge. You keep drinking and you keep talking, just like always. In the meantime, I'll be doing, again as usual.' He paused for emphasis. 'I'll bring Gannon in across his horse by Friday at the outside and after that there'll be no more talk. Problem solved. Good night.'

Murdoch's angry curse followed him out. Kindersley half grinned. A light snow was falling. He was suddenly feeling good. Things were moving and he was making them move. The white peaks were still dimly visible, seeming to float in the darkness. Gannon was out there, but there was no way he could be feeling anything but desperate – cold, hunted and alone.

And in darkness to boot. All that darkness.

By contrast, the badgeman, warm, well-fed and riding high was now on his way to Belle Conway's brightly lighted bordello on Diamond where he intended getting laid without paying one white dime. So, who was winning this final showdown between himself and that cow-pushing loser anyway?

The lights were on at the store on the corner of Diamond as he approached. They always were, for light was their business at Tarryall Lights, Fittings and Fuel. His steps slowed. He didn't want to go in, but of course he did. The storekeeper, his unremarkable face gleaming yellow in the combined glow of a gaudy, leadlight lamp suspended from the ceiling directly above the counter, plus that of several other fine examples of the lampmaker's craft at either end of the counter, greeted him with a gappy grin that was totally genuine.

'Ahh, evenin', Sheriff. What can I do for you tonight?'

Kindersley was perusing the merchandise the way he always did here; it was his favourite place in town and he was a frequent visitor.

He cleared his throat and said gruffly, 'Just checking on my order. It's gone out to my ranch?'

'Sure has, Sheriff. Sent the boy off with it mid afternoon. Two dozen candles, four gallons of coal oil and—'

'I know my own order, damnit.'

'Sorry, Sheriff.' The man hazarded another grin. 'Wouldn't want to offend my best customer, would I?'

But the sheriff wasn't listening. He was gently stroking a quality standard lamp with a purple glass bowl and ochre-colored shade. Then, abruptly, he turned and was gone, leaving the storekeeper running a finger round his shirt collar. He loved to see the sheriff arrive with his billfold, but was invariably relieved when he left, for reasons he didn't fully understand.

It was a two-block walk from the light shop to the discreetly tree-enshrouded brick building with the welcoming crimson lamp above the doorway.

Kindersley walked straight into Belle's by the front door, whereas most clients usually entered more quietly by the side entrances, particularly if they happened to be respectably married family men of town or rangeland. The sheriff had nothing to hide. The law kept a check on the bordello exactly as it did on the saloons, gambling halls and eateries; it was his job.

The perfumed madam appeared immediately to welcome him, was conducting him through the parlour to her private office when a voice, youthful and slightly affected, reached him clearly.

'Well, I'll be goddamned! So this is where you go to get your ashes hauled, is it, Kindersley?'

The room went totally quiet as Kindersley propped. Lonnie Whitney was sprawled on a plush velvet divan with one hand on the bare knee of a scantily clad young woman, the other clutching a glass of amber whiskey.

Belle didn't permit coarse language on her premises, while nobody in his right mind would speak to the sheriff that way.

Yet in the sucked-out moments of silence that followed, neither Kindersley or the madam did anything but stare. Everyone could understand that the madam wouldn't want to come down on Slater Whitney's son; they supposed that likely the same constraints held Kindersley back from hauling Lonnie to his feet and slapping his chops, as he surely would anyone else.

The boy grinned crookedly. 'What's the matter, big man? Come on, you don't have to be bashful. Heck, I hear tell you aren't shy at all when it comes to rolling in the hay when there's a full moon and you're feeling horny—'

'That will be enough, Lonnie.' Belle finally found her voice, and nobody was better skilled at handling trouble with just the right blend of discretion and authority. She took Kindersley's arm, her smile turning brilliant. 'Come, Sheriff, let me offer you something.'

Kindersley's eyes glittered as he allowed himself to be led away. It was only when the office door closed behind them that he let himself go.

'That mouthy little scut! I'll catch him on a dark street some night and I'll bust every bone in his body, by God and by Jesus I will!'

'He's just a spoiled, silly little boy, Boyd. Here, drink this and relax.'

He slugged the whiskey down and returned the glass, drawing the back of his hand across his mouth. The sheriff was back in control, the way he had to be. He nodded at the side door which gave on to the rose-flanked pathway which led from the bordello to the madam's private residence on the adjacent street.

'Everything okay, Belle?' His voice was normal again.

The woman nodded and went to the door, pausing with her hand on the porcelain knob. 'Just relax,' she said again. 'Don't worry about the boy.'

'It's him who should worry about me,' he said tightly, yet managed a grin as he went through. 'Obliged, Belle.'

'You're welcome, Boyd . . . as always.'

Kindersley strode along the curving pathway to reach the rear door of the white-painted cottage. The door was unlocked. He strode directly into a room that was scented, feminine, warm and softly lit. It was a bedroom. The woman sitting up in the bed wore a welcoming smile and nothing else. The sheriff hooked his hat on the elkhorn rack and unbuckled his gunbelt before taking Stella Whitney in his arms.

Gannon knew he was dealing with a pro long before he got to see anything at all in the snow-locked night other than ranch house, outbuildings and empty meadow pastures dreaming under a frozen old moon.

His hands ached from the cold. He could have been long gone with his buffalo robe, camping gear and wallet of old letters and photographs before the nightcomer got anywhere near the headquarters. Yet he was still here. His lips tightened. 'You should be gone, Gannon,' he chided himself aloud. 'Who really cares who the hell it is or what they're doing out here anyway?'

Trouble was, he cared. It was over a year since he'd been a hard-riding, low-tally cowman who spent his days scouring the uplands for wild brush cattle or slogging away on these rough acres daylight to dark. The Whetstone, too remote and poor to attract vandals or campers, had been abandoned and deserted all that time, the stock long wandered away and the shingles tumbling from his roof in the big winds. Today it was worth next to nothing, so what was he trying to prove by lingering on when delay could only prove dangerous? Where was the natural caution he'd always been able to rely on? Had he been living on the dodge so long he was getting to think and act more like a two-gun desperado?

A pebble rattled.

He went low behind the barn door. A rider

approached, a shadowy figure. He drew up and slid down off his horse like a rattlesnake.

Gannon's eyes cut to a single steely gleam. He recognized the lithe figure and that gaudy blanket-coat instantly. So why should he be surprised to see Strummer stalking round his house yard with a revolver in his fist and stealth in his step? Kindersley's ramrod seemed fashioned by nature for this sort of activity. He'd ramrodded the rustling raid and shoot-out on Lazy Y that had seen Gene Dorling shot to death, had played a vital part in the posse's chase after him to Arroyo. It was a sure bet that nothing good had brought him here tonight.

'Gannon!' The voice reached him clearly. 'Come on out, hick. Let's get this over with.'

Gannon's gaze drifted towards the trail. He knew Strummer was just going through the motions with this challenge; force of habit. Kindersley's man was a pro. Had he remotely suspected his presence, Strummer wouldn't have ridden in so openly. Gannon suspected the man had been circling the headquarters for some time before coming on in. But it stood to reason the killer hadn't made this long ride for nothing.

It wasn't long before he discovered what that reason was.

Strummer soon quit prowling. He housed his six-gun and his step showed deliberation as he strode for the house. Digging into the patch-pockets of the blanket coat, he produced paper and something else the watching Gannon couldn't see, until he stuffed the paper under the front door then struck a match.

He was fixing to torch his place!

Right then Gannon knew he had been a fool to linger. He'd told himself he merely wanted to establish the intruder's identity, after which he'd quietly disappear. It was Boyd Kindersley he was after, not his hired help. Now he couldn't go. He'd left it too late. This son of a bitch was fixing to burn his home to the ground, doubtless for no better reason than to deny him a hideaway. So why couldn't he still hightail it? Where was the old reliable and cool-thinking Cole Gannon when you needed him?

It dawned on him that this man no longer existed. Cole Gannon had been uprooted, outlawed, exiled and forced to live with one hand on his gun and eyes in the back of his head for too long. He'd changed. He'd suspected this strongly in the clash with the deputies but was certain of it now.

He was the man Kindersley had made him. So be it. And whoever this new man might be he was rock-solid ready to fight, win and clear his name or go down trying, by God.

He was up.

Snaking out the side door of the barn with a cocked Colt in his fist, Gannon was a stalking shadow as he flitted across to the pumphouse, then, utilizing the cover of the hedge he cut to the end of the porch, just as the wad of paper caught alight.

'Stamp that out or you're a dead man, Strummer.'

Kindersley's man whirled like a startled animal, hand raking holster. Gannon's gun thundered and Strummer ducked beneath the whistling slug, fumbling his draw. Erupting into a headlong charge, Gannon reached the man before he could come clear, catching him with a driving shoulder and ripping a fist into his belly.

Strummer's piece flew one way and he went the other. But even as he hit the boards, he was rebounding with astonishing agility. His sweeping hand knocked Gannon's gun arm down and his head snapped forward as he tried for the head-butt to the face.

Gannon swayed six inches out of harm's way and compressed one whole year of pent-up frustration into another belly rip that had Strummer heaving up his guts and going down like a shot dog.

Gannon's kick drove the man six feet along the boards. He reached him before he stopped rolling, twisted both hands into the lapels of his coat and reefed him to his feet, their faces a bare inch apart, one coldly ferocious, the other ashen and bloodied now.

'You killed Gene, you tried to kill me in Arroyo, and you're still doing Kindersley's dirty work here, you stinking scumsucker,' he panted. 'So tell me, why did he bring me back here?' He shook the man violently. 'Why, varmint? What's his game?'

But Strummer wasn't listening. He was limp in his grasp now, and when released hit the floorboards with a thud like something without bones.

It was a long, taut moment before the fierce light left Gannon's eye, before he stepped back, breathing hard and realizing he'd almost gone too far.

'No,' he panted raggedly, shaking his head as he stepped back to stamp out the sputtering paper wad. He swept up his hat and jammed it on his head. 'They might have put you outside the law, Gannon –

but you're not a killer. Not then or ever. Not that!'

He lunged past the unconscious ramrod and didn't look back as he went out to the draw where the grulla was tied. A muffled stutter of hooves in snow, then all was quiet again on Whetstone Ranch.

6
Of Love and Hate

'I certainly won't be paying that price for any old horse collar, Mr Jay,' Tessa Dorling said firmly, hands on hips in that way she had. 'Three dollars top, take it or leave it.'

The harness-maker faltered. Like many a male around town he simply could never get used to dealing with someone who certainly looked like a woman yet acted, argued and haggled just like a man.

'Okay, Miss Dorling,' he sighed. 'I'll have it finished for you Friday, if that's all right?'

'It will have to be, won't it?' came the terse reply, and Tessa Dorling went outside on to the muddy street to make her way along the plankwalk in the direction of the horseyard where she'd left the buckboard.

For a town prey to all kinds of tensions and uncertainties these days, Tarryall almost had an everyday, relaxed kind of feel about it that overcast morning, with people going about their business, smoke curling lazily from chimney-pots, and good old boys, rugged up to the ears, smoking and yarning on the street corners. The ongoing rustler troubles and Cole Gannon's dramatic return might well remain prime topics at supper tables, store and bar, but today the man in the street seemed simply content to shy clear of drama and just get on with enjoying what so far was shaping as a tolerable kind of day.

But sharp-eyed Tessa was not deceived. She knew Tarryall in all its moods, was very aware that even the most casual looking passer-by was giving her a good eyeing over as she went by. She understood the reason, of course. As a close friend of Gannon's, and privy to what had taken place the night he returned to Lazy Y, she was placed squarely in the eye of the cyclone of conjecture triggered off by his return.

She also knew of the fresh rumor that Sheriff Kindersley was now threatening to lay charges against the Dorlings for harbouring a wanted criminal. She had enemies in town who doubtless would enjoy seeing her appearing anxious and fretful about this, but she would never give them that satisfaction. Although mud-spattered and weather-stained from rescuing a steer trapped in a drift earlier, she was striding it out with arms swinging and head held high when a familiar voice came from the arcade:

'One moment, if you would, m'dear.'

'Something on your mind, Judge?' Her tone was sharp. She had a hundred chores to tend to, not the least of which was keeping an appointment with a man whom Judge Murdoch would most likely hang, given half the chance. But then she half smiled. 'What are you doing lurking around street corners this early in the day? Business down? On the lookout for malefactors to drag into your court, perhaps?' She could tease crusty Murdoch this way; he never seemed to mind.

'Funny you should ask, Missy,' he replied soberly, eyes slanting sideways. 'Matter of fact I was keeping certain parties under surveillance, as you might observe. . . .' His discreet gesture invited Tessa to turn and view two of Tarryall's more recent smoke-and-loaf brigade leaning lazily against the front wall of the law office three doors along. 'Messieurs Hardy and Birch are still with us, you will note, my dear. I've asked you before about these gentlemen, I believe. Have you as yet any notion whom they might be, or what their business is, hmm?'

'I'm sure I haven't, and I think if I did I wouldn't tell you, Judge,' she smiled, moving on. 'A person doesn't know who she can trust in this town anymore – or hadn't you noticed?'

'Female emancipation!' Murdoch snorted disgustedly. Then he narrowed red-rimmed eyes and made his dignified way along the planking before halting, as though by chance, before the blocky redhead and his lean companion with the dark and narrow face. 'Ahh, harrumph . . . morning, gentlemen.'

'Morning, Judge.'

They were polite and inscrutable as always. Or at least it appeared that way to the casual passer-by; or even to someone who might be watching from inside the jailhouse. Linking his hands behind his back and rocking back and forth on his bootheels, Murdoch chatted soberly about the political situation, the odds against the early arrival of the 'humdinger blizzard' the old-timers were predicting, and even the price of a good cigar these days.

Almost anybody who observed this parley taking place would automatically assume that the judge was interrogating this pair whose general nosiness and indolent ubiquity were starting to grate.

Which was exactly the impression he wished to create before he abruptly curtailed the bland discussion to step inside the office, hands locked under the tails of his coat and brows knit tight, the very picture of a sober gentleman with serious matters on his mind.

'Well?' growled Kindersley, leaning back in his big buffalo-hide desk chair. 'I saw you talking to them.'

'As ordered,' said the judge, extending his hands over the pot-belly stove. 'By you,' he reminded tartly.

'Never mind the flapdoodle. What'd you find out?'

Kindersley simply couldn't relax about Hardy and Birch, the judge reflected. Small wonder. Triggered off by his plummeting unpopularity, the sheriff was wary of everybody these days. His suspicions of this pair, as confided to Murdoch, ranged from cow-thieves themselves perhaps, to possibly range detectives, newsmen or even undercover lawmen assigned to investigate his failure against the rustlings. This made him even more difficult to get along with than usual, which was going some.

The judge took his time replying.

Although Kindersley appeared his normal robust self today, you could never be sure these days. More often than not this former two-man team who'd worked so effectively together to clean up Tarryall, simply didn't get along anymore. The sheriff might attribute this to the judge's drinking, but Murdoch knew the real reason. The sheriff had changed vastly over the past year or so. Everybody said so. There were times when the judge wasn't sure if he was dealing with an ally or an enemy. Was it any wonder a man hit the whiskey?

'Not a thing,' he muttered finally. 'And I still believe your suspicions are unfounded.' He wrung his hands for warmth over the heat. As always the law office smelt strongly of coal oil and candlewax. Mostly the lamps burned all night here – sheriff's orders. Murdoch cleared his throat. 'So, how's your ramrod today, Sheriff? I hear tell he's . . . indisposed.'

'Strummer's doing just fine. Spill off his horse is all.' Their eyes locked. Murdoch could always tell when the sheriff was lying. 'Well, old man, don't you have an appointment?'

'You should know, Sheriff, seeing as you set it up. But I'd still like to know why you want me to see Whitney today.'

'I thought that would be plain enough.' Kindersley heaved himself erect and began prowling the confines of the office, restless and hard faced. 'You know very well the man doesn't consult with me any more, and I know for a fact he holds me personally responsible for his problems. Damnit all, the last time we talked Whitney had the hide to half hint that I could clean up those rustlers if I really wanted. Now what in hell do you suppose he meant by that?'

'I have no idea. Mr Whitney does not confide in me any more than he does in you, although he once did. But I still don't know exactly what you expect to come of a meeting.'

Kindersley made an impatient gesture.

'Over recent weeks I feel I've lost contact with High T altogether, and in that vacuum I've developed a hunch Mr Big might be cooking up something underhanded, something I'm not supposed to know about. Hell! Could even be something aimed at me; that's how hostile he's got about his lousy cows.'

He paused to light a crooked-back cigar. The judge knew this frame of mind. It was Boyd Kindersley in his one-against-the-world mood. It had stood him in good stead against the wild men and the outlaws, but this was different. The potential adversary here was one of the kings of the county.

'Well, we haven't done as well as might be expected—'

'That's just what I need from you,' Kindersley cut him off. 'One hundred per cent support. Not! Well, to blazes with you, Judge. You just do what you're paid for and I'll handle the rest. Now, I reckon Whitney's set himself up here in town with purposes I'm not going to like, so your job is to find out what they are. Is that plain enough for you?'

Time was when Judge Cletus Murdoch would not permit any man to speak to him this way. But that was too many bottles ago. Yet he salvaged enough spirit from his better years for a parting shot as he made to leave.

'You seem certain Whitney is hatching up something, Sheriff, not just to suspect it. Mind telling me your source of information on that score?'

Kindersley's face turned dark. 'Get the hell out of here, you booze-soaked old fraud!'

Murdoch smiled grimly as he left. His barb had hit home. But the grin quickly faded. If the rumors about Kindersley and Whitney's wife were true, was it possible that other even uglier whispers about the once venerated lawman might also have some basis in fact?

That was a question he'd been forced to ask himself with ever-increasing frequency, until he'd finally been driven to dig deep and try to resurrect his sense of morality and honor, as well as the courage he'd feared drowned forever in blended whiskey.

Thus rearmed, he'd done what any decent Justice of the People would when faced with such a dilemma.

Secretly and fearfully, the judge had initiated steps calculated to solve the many mysteries of Fall River County. He'd been running scared ever since. He dared confide in nobody. He was a man alone, and quite likely playing with death. And yet – by God and by Jesus – when he wasn't drowning in a bottle, it felt almost good!

The judge turned the beaver-fur collar of his old-fashioned coat high around his ears and headed for the mansion, only to find himself retracing his steps just a few minutes later. Whitney had cancelled their meeting claiming 'family' concerns, the message delivered at the front door by a footman. Murdoch was in foul temper as he stomped along, feeling he'd been dismissed like some kind of lackey. But he was doing the big man an injustice. The colonel did in truth have family concerns that morning. Major concerns.

Waiting for his wife to come downstairs, Slater Whitney strolled through his town house where everything was quiet and still.

The place he'd built along the lines of an antebellum Southern mansion, with majestic columns and an air of solid grandeur, was not yet old but was built to last, to impart a sense of permanency. And that was the way the rich man liked to think of the edifice. Permanent. A fitting place for him and his wife to spend their winters away from the spread; to enjoy what there was of a social season in Tarryall; entertain their wealthy friends and, most important of all, get to focus on family life with their son.

He paused just inside the entrance of what he called the 'war room', smiling as he thought about his son and heir and the pride of his life. He had been crazy about Lonnie since the day he was born, this unique bond seeming to strengthen and even deepen during the past year as the High T suffered crisis after crisis – and the Whitney marriage began to falter.

The smile faded as he circled the room which smelled richly of leather and waxed oak. The walls were hung with pictures and memorabilia of the War Between the States, some immortalizing the colonel's not insignificant part in the great campaigns.

For once he seemed unaware of crossed sabres and regimental colours. He'd come to Tarryall to relax yet was taut as a guitar string today, incapable of not dwelling upon his adversities: the potentially ruinous drain on the spread which was the foundation of his fortune, the no longer unbelievable whispers and rumors concerning his lady wife.

The colonel was under siege and was acutely aware this quiet morning that everything he possessed and valued was in some kind of jeopardy. Yet he still managed to retain his authoritative poise even when his wife entered the room looking puffy-faced and petulant, still in night robe and mules.

'Good-morning, my dear.' The colonel could be intimidating in his suppressed rages. Exquisitely polite, as befitted an officer and gentleman, but to those who knew him well the ice and fire were detectable just below the surface.

Stella Whitney carelessly tightened the sash of her crimson robe then dropped into a plush chair at the head of the long, teak table and plucked a cigarette from a cedar box. Smoking was just another habit his wife had acquired of which Whitney disapproved, but was by no means the most undesirable on that long list. She lighted up with a silver pocket-flint, drew deep and leaned back, still a handsome woman at forty but slowly losing her bloom.

'Well, come on, out with it, darling,' she said in a bored voice. 'What have I done wrong now? And don't say nothing. I'm your wife, remember? I know all your moods and—'

'Kindersley.'

The woman's face showed surprise. She had not expected him to be so direct.

'What about Boyd?' she challenged. Then, before he could respond. 'No, wait a minute. Why should you always get to set the debate agenda, Colonel! Why don't we discuss your not allowing your wife to buy that beautiful gown she saw in Gilbert's yesterday? And all the other times she's been in desperate need and you refused her throughout the summer, and all the summers and winters before. Let's discuss your lousy, penny-pinching ways that would drive any woman to drink, *darling*!'

'It has to stop!'

She leaned forward, the robe gapping to reveal the tops of her breasts.

'What does, Slater? Come on, don't hedge around it that way you always do. Put it in plain words even your wife can understand. What is it that must stop?'

'Damn you, Stella!' he exploded, openly angry at last. 'You know what I'm saying. Your seeing Kindersley. The dogs are barking it and I damn well won't have it, do you hear. I won't have my son's mother flaunting herself around with another man, much less that fellow, by God!'

'Oh, your son's mother am I now?' she flared, jumping to her feet. 'Not your wife. Lonnie's immaculate mother. And that's all you care about, isn't it? You couldn't care less if I was rolling in the hay with half the county providing your precious little tin god son wasn't upset or didn't get to hear about it.'

'Don't talk that way, Stella. It's so common.'

'Common, am I? You haven't seen common, Mister Colonel High-and-Mighty Whitney! I can out-common better than you can out-snob, and by heaven that is saying something. Now you listen to me. . . .'

The angry voices washing from the room carried

clearly to the foot of the great staircase where the boy stood listening, with one hand resting upon the newel post and his face white with shock and disbelief. He wanted to rush into the war room and silence his mother and comfort his father but found he couldn't move, as the quarrel went on and on.

Down from the mesa lands south-west of the Pawnee Trail, the solitary horseman in the black buffalo-robe coat with the carbine resting across his saddle pommel rode slowly towards the meeting place.

Cole Gannon knew he was riding High T dirt now even though the line markers lay hidden beneath the snow. This was well above Lazy Y and the Keelock Hills ranches, tucked away beneath the mighty overhang of the Iron Comb escarpment which provided bad-weather shelter for this sweep of highly prized winter grazeland of Slater Whitney's upland pastures.

The High T boss had the happy knack of turning everything he touched into gold. The Iron Comb region was a good example. When winter set in properly in the Nacimientos and the blizzards finally came raging and shrieking up from the bottomless bowels of their ice caverns in the deep and secret heart of the mighty mountains to burst across the Sangre ranchlands, it was a fierce struggle just to keep your herds alive as rancher Gannon well knew. But here there was ample grass, good water and shelter to be had in even the worst weather, and if a rancher could meet the price charged by the High T he could avail himself of the grazeland until the big freeze blew over.

Although hundreds of cattle were to be seen grazing placidly across the slopes today, Gannon, invisible within the cover of the pine woods above as he pushed the big grulla southwards, noted two puzzling facts with his trained cowman's eye.

One, there wasn't a solitary High T herder to be seen. And two, he didn't see a single beast wearing the Whitney brand.

How come?

He shook his head. There were too many questions and too few answers already without adding to the list. He pushed on faster, following a long tangent which took him well beyond the herds to a remote section of thorn and brush country until he eventually reached the natural clearing in the woods and the frozen pond encircled by firs which was his destination.

He swung down stiffly and circled the clearing, swinging his arms and breathing fog gusts into the air. Halting to dig for his tobacco, he lifted a hand to his face to finger a bruised cheekbone. He grimaced, then concentrated on fashioning a cigarette. He was hurting some but there was satisfaction in the knowledge that Strummer would be hurting a hell of a lot more.

He lit up, eyes distant and remote. Often, during quiet spells down along the Hondo he'd found it difficult to think of himself as a fugitive on the run and no longer a simple rancher whose only concern was for his cattle. But after last night he supposed he fitted the role well enough. The fugitive-cum-desperado Gannon had sure been uppermost last night when he went for Kindersley's ramrod like a she-bear protecting her young. He'd have killed Strummer if he'd had to and likely not lost much sleep over it either. That was just how much he had changed.

'Thanks a bunch, Kindersley,' he said bitterly. 'But payback time is coming.'

He had to go on believing that. He'd returned home hoping to help his friends, but knew now he was staying on to both clear his name and square accounts as well. Cole Gannon wouldn't be returning to life on the dodge a second time. He'd keep on after Kindersley until the day he could bring him to trial before Judge Murdoch, or go down trying. Yet even to his own ear this sounded more like the defiant brag of a hellion than the considered statement of a law-abiding citizen.

He glanced at the pool, their secret spot which he and the Dorlings, brother and sister, had visited for lazy summer swimming and picnics which seemed to last forever – maybe a hundred years ago.

The grulla whickered and lifted its head, bringing Gannon swivelling around with the .45 in his gloved hand, facing back the way he'd come.

Moments later Tessa appeared from the trees. She was riding her cart-horse barebacked and swung down as lithely as an Indian. Their arrangement to meet up here had been made prior to the incident at the Whetstone. Tessa showed sudden shock at sight of his marked-up face, came towards him quickly then hesitated, almost awkwardly. This place was rich in memories for her also, but so much had changed, maybe too much.

'What happened?' she asked quietly, pausing to

knock clods of mud from her heavy workboots against a rock. He told her and she grimaced. 'So they tried to burn you down.' She shrugged. 'I guess we can take this as a sign that the sheriff has taken the gloves off and is going after you come hell or high water. That how you see it, Cole?'

He nodded. All along, he and the Dorlings were aware that the most dangerous outlaw in Fall River County was Boyd Kindersley. But there had been no chance of proving that before, and little now, or so it would seem. Yet this was the purpose behind their meeting: to swap knowledge and ideas and hopefully come up with a working plan upon which to base the campaign of the Dorlings and Cole Gannon vs. The Rest.

Their conversation roamed widely afield as they sat by the pool and it was some time before he realized Tessa was continually breaking off to stare around at the trees as though expecting some interruption. The last time she did this he reached out and touched her shoulder, intending only to attract her attention. But she flinched sharply and jumped up, a guilty flush immediately staining her cheeks as he stared up at her in puzzlement.

'What the tarnation, Tess . . .' he said, rising. 'You scared of me or something?'

She shook her head violently. It was so unusual to see this woman at a disadvantage. Nowadays, that was. Before the trouble she had been different, softer, gentle even. The intervening twelve months had changed her as greatly as it had him.

'I'm sorry, Cole. I didn't mean to jump.' She shrugged. 'It's the tension, I guess. The truth is I'm a little nervous today. You see, I got a feeling halfway out here that I might have picked up a tail from town. Do you think we should go take a look, just in case?'

He sure as hell did.

By the time they quit the encircling woods to reach a lookout point, the wind was rising. With the escarpment looming mightily overhead, and cows grazing placidly on all sides, this High T pasture appeared as pretty and tranquil as a perfect colour picture on a serum company calendar. But with field-glasses constantly to his eyes and sweeping the lower regions in the direction of the town trail, Gannon was in no way reassured. He realized he had no reason to be when he finally sighted what he was looking for, yet had hoped not to see.

It was just a flickering glance at first, but enough. Two horsemen were climbing towards them along the snow-banked trace of Sycamore Creek.

Wordlessly he passed Tessa the glasses, then began checking his gun.

'I can't identify them positively at this distance,' she said, 'but it's just possible they might be those two men I told you of who've been hanging around and trying to make contact with me lately, Hardy and B—' she broke off sharply. 'Cole, what are you doing?'

It seemed pretty obvious but he felt obliged to explain. 'It's time,' he said with a look she scarcely recognized. 'We've let people get away with murdering us and busting up our lives and wrecking our ranches and treating us like trash for too long.' He nodded grimly as he put the six-gun away then whipped the carbine from its stiff leather scabbard. 'These varmints are tailing you like they feel they've got the right, or something. Well that right's cancelled, if it ever existed. You wait here, girl, I'm going down to check out their credentials.'

Alarmed, Tessa impulsively reached out and grabbed his arm; no fear of physical contact now.

'Cole, don't talk this way. You look awful. Please calm down and think on it before you do anything foolish.'

He stared down at the hand on his arm, then into her eyes, remembering how boy-and-girl easy together they had been when Gene was alive and the world seemed a cleaner, more innocent place. Remembering just how much they had lost . . . remembering every day of a long and lonesome year that had made him over into the kind of man he'd never wanted to be.

Then the moment was gone, willed away. If he was what others had made him then he was not about to waste those combative skills he'd been forced to acquire. Not now when they were needed, he wasn't.

'These jaspers are mine,' he said tersely and went heeling away, barely hearing her call after him above the sound of his horse.

By contrast, he made no more sound than a drifting snow shadow as he entered the sycamores on foot a half mile below the escarpment. Carbine at the ready, he snaked between gaunt trunks as the sounds of the running water reached him. He slipped into a low crouch and now could see the creek as it cut its way between white rocks and stiffened brush. He ducked behind a deadfall at the sound of labouring horses.

The carbine hammer clicked back silently. In that waiting moment before the bobbing heads of horses appeared through the fork of a sycamore, rancher Cole Gannon knew he was ready to kill if he must. He was sickened by the thought but knew he wouldn't turn away from his appointed course now because he could not.

Two men rode into clear sight, one husky in a plaid coat, his companion slender and dark astride a black horse. He'd never seen them before, yet was certain of two things. They looked dangerous, and were plainly following Tessa's sign. That was all he needed to know as he raised the carbine, his sudden shout sounding sharp as a gunshot.

'Freeze, or you're dead!'

7
'Reach!'

The steely scent of danger was in the air.

It was there in the iron set of Cole Gannon's stubbled jaw as he watched his two-man catch over his gunsights; it came off strongly from the taut and forward-leaning figures of the men on horseback with hands suspended motionless above gun handles, as though time and motion had been frozen. It was emphasized by the stamp and jingle of nervous horses and the now sinister-sounding burble of Sycamore Creek in its rocky bed.

'Get those paws up or I'll start in shooting. I mean it!'

It seemed to cause them actual physical pain for Hardy and Birch to raise empty hands to shoulder height. For these were men trained to respond in situations like this, taught not to get jumped like rubes from Rubesville. Submission was anathema to them. Yet both continued to claw even higher in response to an upwards flick of that dark muzzle. For Tarryall's mystery men were also highly skilled in assessing people, and instinct warned that this shadowy rifleman sounded like a man who'd do exactly as he said.

They sat their saddles stone-faced and impotent as Gannon emerged from cover to look them over at close quarters. It was only when they saw his face clearly that they gaped in astonishment, almost as if in recognition. Tall build, fair-headed, square-jawed with light-colored eyes. They traded glances and Wes Hardy breathed, 'Do you reckon. . . ?'

'Could be,' replied Birch.

'Did I say you could talk?' Gannon's voice cracked. Something was busting loose inside him as he confronted yet more people he took to be enemies – like the goddamn woods were full of them. 'You!' he growled, indicating Hardy. 'Get down and shuck your gun-belt. Then you can tell me why you're hunting a decent woman, you lousy sons of bitches.'

Hardy obeyed promptly, but couldn't hold back as he slid to ground. 'Olan, I'm certain it's him now . . . gotta be.' Then before Gannon could silence him, 'Mister, you wouldn't be Cole Gannon of Whetstone Ranch by any chance?'

'You're right, by God! It is him,' gasped Birch. He began lowering his hands but shot them up again as the carbine twitched again. He hazarded a placatory grin. 'Mr Gannon – and we know it's got to be from our picture – you've got this the wrong way round. We didn't mean Miss Dorling any harm. It's only because we hoped she might lead us to you that we were tagging her. Why don't you put that weapon up and let us explain.' He spread his hands while still keeping them well above his head. 'Mister, we're your friends. Birch and me are the law.'

'Yeah, you sure look it,' Gannon retorted. His voice was still rough-edged yet some of the hunted fierceness was leaving his eyes. Motioning the second man to step down, he waited until both had shucked their gun-belts and backed away from them before lowering his weapon fractionally. He searched their faces. They were tough faces yet strong and maybe even halfway reassuring, he realized now.

But he still wasn't taking any chances. 'Convince me,' he said, raising a booted foot to a deadfall. 'Let me have it fast and straight.'

Seemed a reasonable enough demand under the circumstances. Nonetheless, Hardy and Birch delayed long enough to give one another a searching look. They had reasons for wariness their captor couldn't even begin to guess at. Gannon swore and flicked his carbine again, and it was patently plain that hesitancy was not an option.

'Okay,' redheaded Hardy sighed, and folding his arms began to talk. He spoke so easily and eloquently that it wasn't all that long before Gannon began to grudgingly suspect he might well be telling the truth.

Their story went like this:

They were agent-operatives attached to a quasi-secret government security unit known as the Bureau of Investigations, which had its headquarters in Santa Fe and whose charter from Washington empowered its highly trained personnel to conduct a wide range of investigative operations which, for whatever reason, were deemed to be beyond the capabilities of regular law enforcement.

One of the Bureau's most frequent areas of operation, Hardy explained while studying Gannon's reaction, was corruption and illegality in governmental agencies ranging from the US Army through the court system all the way down through territorial and county instrumentalities and authorities. There was specific emphasis on all areas of law enforcement.

Here Hardy paused momentarily as he finally began to relax some. Plainly they had Gannon's undivided attention now, and were encouraged.

'Thought that would grab you, Gannon,' Birch said with a hesitant grin.

'Why so?' Gannon was surely interested but still far from sold.

'That'll become clear as we go along,' Hardy assured. 'Olan.' His nod handed the ball to Birch, who quietly proceeded to work his way towards delivery of the stunner.

The agents had been assigned duty in Fall River County primarily to investigate the rustling attacks against High T Ranch, as well as the murder of Gene Dorling.

Gannon's expression sharpened but he didn't interrupt.

Their assignment had come at the behest of the county commissioner in the capital, who in turn was responding to an urgent plea for help which reached the Bureau through a third party in Tarryall acting for the most obvious and influential of supplicants in this region, namely Colonel Slater Whitney himself.

But in Tarryall the agents promptly ran into a

brick wall of silence, suspicion and even outright hostility, most of the latter emanating from Boyd Kindersley's law office. Indeed, so poor had their progress been in the face of this opposition that they had been in danger of being recalled when Gannon showed. The man then proceeded to explain just why this was so significant.

The operatives' exhaustive briefing for the Tarryall assignment had encompassed all material, evidence and hearsay associated with Fall River County's rustling operations dating back to the first raid. Naturally this covered in considerable detail the murder of Gene Dorling and the subsequent pursuit of Gannon, the man identified as his killer.

'It was only after the Federal Legal Department was called in to examine all material relevant to the entire Dorling–Gannon–Kindersley affair that momentous decisions were reached in a court of law which are vitally important to you personally, Gannon,' Birch stated.

'Explain,' he grunted.

'As you may be aware, following your escape from the posse a year ago you were tried *in absentia* here in Tarryall and found guilty of murder in the first degree?'

He nodded grimly. Knew all about that so-called trial. Along with the $500 reward posted for his capture. Dead or alive.

'We have some of the finest legal brains in the country working in our investigative authority, Mr Gannon. When serious doubts about Sheriff Kindersley were first aroused by his glaring inability to prevent Colonel Whitney's stock losses, the authority eventually turned its focus to your trial. The transcript was examined in minute detail and, just before we were dispatched here, they handed down their finding.'

Gannon wasn't acting diffident any longer. His mouth was dry and his pulse was quicker. 'And?'

'It is the considered opinion of the authority – which for your reassurance works under the auspices of the western arm of the Supreme Court – that the evidence presented against you was fatally flawed. In other words, Mr Gannon, we believe that were you to be retried for the alleged murder of Gene Dorling today, you would be found innocent. And that is official.'

Gannon showed no reaction. It was all internal. He was acutely aware of the thud of his heart. The big ganglion of nerves in his solar plexus twitched as the impact of what he was hearing rammed home.

Officially innocent!

Surely this was impossible. Yet glancing from a smiling Birch to a soberly nodding Hardy, he knew he desperately wanted to accept these men for what they claimed to be and to believe that what they were saying – the incredible thing they were saying – was nothing but the truth.

'Well, man?' Hardy said when the silence dragged on. 'Surely you understand what we're telling you? Don't you have anything to say?'

He certainly did. 'Let me see your identification, right now.' He knew deep down he believed now. But he couldn't risk being wrong. A man could only take so much.

His reaction didn't appear to bother the men.

They promptly produced a leather document wallet from Birch's saddle-bag which contained enough evidence of identity to convince even a hanging judge. By the time he was through with the material, Gannon had dismounted and his carbine now leaned against a tree. He stood shaking his head as he studied pages of script, many bearing waxed governmental seals.

Until that moment he hadn't realized the sun had come out and the snow was melting.

Just a few hours earlier, cold and exhausted after a long night spent in the musty blackness of an old bear cave, his spirits were low and his optimism running out. The Lazy Y shoot-out, Kindersley more powerful than ever, the ruckus with Strummer at the spread: too damned much. Surely?

Now he was soaring. Hardy and Birch were surely the hitherto unsuspected element that was desperately needed to lend him fresh heart and maybe even offer the support he needed to hold his own against the enemy.

Under different circumstances he knew it would have taken far longer for them to trust one another. But time was encapsulated here. He needed them and they seemed to need him at least as much. So the fugitive hazarded a smile that was immediately mirrored in two relieved faces, and suddenly the little creek burbling by didn't sound sinister any longer.

Then Hardy was speaking again.

'You should know, Gannon, that so important was the uncovering of this evidence at the time, that our first designated assignment was to find you, wherever you might be. But within a fcw days there were rustling raids against High T and Lazy Y and our superiors instead re-assigned us here.'

'So, what a coincidence that you should show right at this time, huh?' commented Birch.

There was something here that Gannon felt warranted closer consideration. Something important. But his concentration was abruptly broken by the sound of a faint clatter of hoof against stone from up slope. Gannon whipped out his Colt and went low, the noticeably slower agents following suit.

Tessa rode from the sycamores looking both peeved and suspicious.

Gannon grinned. He couldn't help it. Worlds might collide and empires fall, but a woman was still a woman. And Tessa had always been her own kind of woman in a man's world as she'd just demonstrated yet again.

Turned out he'd offended without knowing it by ordering her to stay put while he rode off, 'manlike' as she put it, to confront a perceived danger.

What gave him the notion she wasn't perfectly capable of looking out for herself?

It didn't help any when an almost light-hearted Gannon and two animated strangers couldn't help but bust out grinning. They weren't laughing at her; all three were still simply intensely relieved they'd managed to stumble into contact almost at what might be the eleventh hour. For all of them.

Even so, levity was a a big mistake. Gannon had to move fast to grab the headstall of Tessa's horse as she made to heel away across the creek with her lips compressed and back rigid, a woman fighting her battles in a man's world first, and Cole Gannon's friend second.

'Hey, easy, Tess, easy,' he panted, swallowing his smile. 'You don't understand, girl. Will you just get down and let us explain before you go jumping the gun? There's news, Tess,' he said, indicating his mint-new friends. 'The best of news, that you're going to be crazy to hear.'

'Indeed?' she said crossly, yet allowed him to hand her down anyway. But once seated upon the deadfall, with Gannon behind her as Hardy and Birch continued their story, there was no way Tessa Dorling could have moved even had she wanted. Gannon neither.

The revelations they'd made concerning his altered status in the eyes of New Mexican law was only part of the wider picture, as the agents now felt confident enough to reveal. For their prime objective in being assigned duty in Tarryall had not been to find Gannon – desperately vital though this was – rather to investigate Sheriff Kindersley.

The belated discovery that Kindersley had presented a corrupt case against Gannon before Judge Murdoch, coming as it did on the heels of Slater Whitney's urgent request for help from the authorities, had turned the spotlight of the Bureau's attentions upon the law officer. As a direct result of this, Hardy and Birch were despatched to Tarryall to both investigate the rustlings at first hand and to examine the interlocking administrations of Kindersley and the judge.

Three weeks on found Hardy and Birch

convinced that Kindersley could well be some kind of rogue bull lawman, a man maybe grown too large on power, arrogance and ambition. Somehow the lawman had managed to acquire his own ranch on a lawman's low salary. He appeared to exert total control over the courthouse, was widely accused of employing excessive force and even overt brutality in the execution of his duty. He was at loggerheads with Slater Whitney, and the agents further believed him to be involved in an affair with the rich man's wife.

'Which all adds up to exactly zero, from a legal point of view,' Birch said soberly. 'Thus far we haven't been able to come up with anything against Kindersley that would stand up in a court of law. As a consequence, we could still be hauled off this assignment despite all our suspicions and despite having made contact with you at last, Gannon.'

'Well at least I suppose it was lucky you gentlemen decided I might lead you to Cole,' Tessa put in. 'But can he help you? I mean, really help?'

'That remains to be seen.' Hardy was on his feet facing Gannon now, his manner sober. 'You're number one on Kindersley's wanted list, and he's also highly suspicious of us. What he doesn't know is that we've made contact, and that could work in our favour. I know you're relieved about your legal position, and you'd have to be buoyed up now you're aware official suspicion is directed at the sheriff. But the truth of the situation is that right now at this moment, even united, we four pose no real threat to Kindersley. He's still holding all the cards. He tamed Tarryall and he still rules town and courthouse. The man looks almost impregnable. Also, Olan and I have a hunch something is building up in town, something dangerous and maybe unstoppable, which the sheriff is up to his neck in. The signs are all there. Tension's thick enough to cut with a knife in there right now. . . .'

He paused, seemingly depressed by his own words. He shrugged. 'Which is why we'd best be getting back.'

'We'll maintain contact through you, Miss Dorling,' Birch said. 'So, what are your immediate plans, Cole? We suggest you lay low and keep out of trouble. Matter of fact we insist on it. Kindersley wants you desperately. But in the final wrap-up, if we fail to nail him with anything else, you could prove to be the last ace we have to play against him. You'll leave this to us?'

'I'll think on it.' Gannon was the quiet and considering cowman again in that moment, but the hard-jawed fugitive from the law was lurking close. This meeting with the agents was heady stuff. But he was still his own man.

Tessa brushed back a strand of hair and, realizing how thin and worn she looked, was reminded of his priorities.

He handed the woman up from the deadfall and guided her to her horse.

'A big day and a great one, gentlemen. And don't fret. With what you've revealed today I know we're going to take Kindersley down. I want everybody to believe that.' He paused to throw a salute. 'Until next time.'

A wolf began howling towards Stranger's

Mountain as the party broke up. It was a ghostly sound and lonesome.

Gannon felt relieved as he escorted Tessa back to the ridge, brimming with plans stemming from the meeting with the agents. But he would be careful, he assured himself. He planned to spend time contacting old friends and keeping watch on developments both in Tarryall and out on the range with emphasis on High T and the Kindersley spread.

His good mood should have proven infectious. Nonetheless, Tessa was strangely silent and withdrawn throughout the short ride, finding it difficult to raise a confident smile as they parted at a high bend in the trail with plans to rendezvous the following day.

She told herself it wasn't a matter of loyalty or confidence here; it was simply that she seemed to have a far stronger fear of Boyd Kindersley than did the trio, and couldn't envision him 'going down' before three men, or ten times that many.

Maybe when it was all boiled down, she just knew the sheriff better than any of them, Cole included.

The sun was less bright than before. Within the last hour clouds had rolled up over the divide and were spilling out across the sky. The air seemed unusually warm and heavy and the wind had died away to usher in an unnatural stillness which Tessa found strangely oppressive. Coming atop her attack of pessimism, this caused her to slip into what her grouchy old father might call one of her 'moods'.

Life had been brutally hard on this woman since the death of her brother and Gannon's flight.

Where for years she had been free to rely upon father, brother and friend, suddenly she found herself running a cow ranch single handed and caring for an increasingly dependent father, expected to cope stoically with rustling, isolation and the threat of ultimate failure.

She'd survived. But the cost was high. Some called her 'Miss Britches' in town where she knew she was widely regarded as mannish and unfeminine. Often she felt she had grown shrewish and difficult. Which was exactly the way she felt when she got home only to find the milch cows had gotten loose during her absence and her father complaining because he hadn't had a proper lunch.

Tessa managed to hold her tongue as she slapped bacon into a skillet before going to tend the cows. Old Perce watched her closely from his chair; he'd failed a great deal but his brain and eye were still sharp.

'So,' he said after a taut silence, 'how is he today anyhow?'

She glanced up from the cook stove. 'Who do you mean?'

'Who else would I mean, girl? Cole, of course.'

She couldn't conceal her surprise. 'How did you know? I mean, who says I saw Cole?'

His knowing smirk was offensive. 'I can always tell. Always could for that matter. You never had to tell me whenever you'd bumped into him in town, or if you and Gene had been off doin' chores with him. Plain as cheap paint, so it was. Always.'

She flipped the bacon over in the pan. 'My God you talk some rot, you really do.'

'So deny it then if I'm mistook, Miss Bossy. Deny you ain't got that colour in your cheeks because you've been meetin' up with your old beau. Go ahead. Hey, where you goin'?'

'Where does it look like? Outside!' She swept by him but paused for a parting shot from the doorway. 'Your flies are undone, old man.'

She was gone. Dorling looked down. He was buttoned up tight. He cursed, red-faced, but there was none to hear. And he wondered, yet again, just what kind of God would take your only son, rob you of your health then leave you dependent on a girl who could sometimes act meaner than a stick-poked polecat.

8

The Sheriff's Head

The sheriff had bad dreams.

It was only at night when he slept, either out at the ranch or here in the back room of the jailhouse, that he ever proved vulnerable to the kind of fears and terrors that troubled lesser men. Awake, Boyd Kindersley seemed impervious to all anxiety, uncertainty or the everyday weaknesses to which humanity is prone.

Only the dreams reined him back to the herd. Of course he hated and secretly feared them. But there was nothing he could do about them, worming their way into his sleeping subconscious as they did.

And that night it was the childhood nightmare, that old familiar which he hated worst of all. . . .

He awoke in a sweat, jerking up in his bunk bed in long johns and undershirt, wide-eyed and lathered in sweat. Normally the jailhouse was quiet this time of day, but as he grew aware of arguing voices from up front he realized it was this that had awakened him.

He should have been grateful to be rescued from his dream. But that was not how the sheriff of Tarryall was put together. He didn't think in terms of gratitude. Not ever. In most ways that counted, he was different from other men, fashioned from another template.

Dragging a straight-edge razor across his heavy jaw before the tiny square of mirror in the adjacent washroom, the sheriff did what he did every morning of his life during this small ritual.

He planned his day and assessed his situation.

Today, perhaps more so than any single day since first pinning on the star, this proved a major challenge. For on this day, in the secret world of the sheriff's head, there was a psychic awareness of events coming to a head, rushing headlong towards resolution.

The man who had bad dreams compensated by dreaming high, wide and handsome when awake. Whilst working for wages of one hundred a month plus fine fees, he dreamed of vast and rolling rangelands studded with prime cattle wearing the bold BK brand, of herds of thoroughbred horses grazing his grassy meadows; of mansions and wealth and the acclaim in public places which such success in life entailed.

It is a fact of life that millions dream that way. The difference between the gray masses and the sheriff of Tarryall was that he had been working long and often dangerously to transform dreams into bedrock reality, and very soon, possibly even this week, could well get to see them realized.

Providing he held his nerve and didn't flinch

when hard decisions had to be made, of course. The game was afoot, so he assured his clean-shaven image in the mirror glass. Sure, there might well be hitches now, threats and obstacles he had not envisioned before. Yet his planning had been sound and his nerve had held. He'd acted swiftly and decisively in response to every threat, and now that the final battle was at hand he found himself exhilarated by the prospect of action, the pungent whiff of gunsmoke.

Who cared about bad dreams?

Fully dressed, with rust-coloured hair tamed by brush and water and the big guns riding his hips, the sheriff of Tarryall felt complete as he swept his Stetson off the rack before turning to get the lights.

Three oil lamps glowed softly all night long in the jailhouse's rear room, while a fourth, much larger, fashioned from brass with a coloured glass bowl, hung suspended from the rafters by a long silver chain to illuminate the front office.

It was the deputies' duty to light the lamps in the evenings but mostly they were left to the sheriff to douse in the mornings. Fastidious about his lights and lighting was the peacekeeper, who even drove about in a rubber-tyred racing buggy equipped with four handsome brass-bound riding lamps. And, as people noted, he invariably drove fast.

The simple chore completed he made his way along the passageway between the cells to reach the front office just as his junior deputy was beginning to get flustered.

'Damnit, cowboy,' he was saying, 'nobody's stole none of your money. I cleaned out your pockets personal when we locked you up last night, and it's all here, every cent.'

'The hell you say,' barked the drifter across the desk. 'I been clipped and—'

'What is this?'

The stranger had not heard Kindersley enter the room. He whirled. He was stubby as a sawed-off shotgun and looked about as dangerous. Peeved also.

'About time you showed your face, badgeman,' he said aggressively. He was new-come to town and unaware just how things worked here. 'I been robbed by your deputy and I want it back, all of it.'

'Get your ass out of here while you can still walk.'

Kindersley's tone was mild but the deputy was not deceived. He knew his superior in all his moods, knew the sheriff was riding in danger mode. Kindersley recognized this fact also. He was feeling good, but edgy. Like, real edgy.

'Why you top-lofty sonuva—' the red-faced waddy snarled. Then he tried something few sane men in Fall River County would dream of. He swung one at the sheriff's head.

The man never saw the pistoning knee that drove into his drum gut. He buckled in the middle, his face a sudden awful gray. Swinging his right arm high, Kindersley brought the clenched forearm smashing down on the unprotected neck with savage force. The troublemaker hit the floor like a slab of meat, and next moment was given the bum's rush through the doors and flung clear across the porch to wrap around the hitch rail, where he was left hanging like a mess of dirty laundry.

Pawnee Street froze.

They might be well familiar with their sheriff's vigorous style of law enforcement, but this brutal display before the day got properly under way seemed excessive.

But the moment Kindersley swept the street with his gaze everyone came unlocked, and the citizens were hustling about their business again as he returned inside to meet the deputy's pop-eyed stare.

'Something on your mind, son?' The sheriff was hard, yet rarely this extreme; someone was calling for the medic outside. But then, this was a special kind of day. The day he must draw all his strings together in his big fist – and damnation to any man who sought to impede him, beginning with a nameless bum who dared cross him up. He shot his shirtcuffs and straightened his string tie as the young man stood awkwardly, going from one foot to another. 'No? Then be about your business.'

The man gulped but stood his ground. 'Permission to report on an important matter, Sheriff.'

Kindersley was closing the charge book. 'What?'

'Please, sir, you should know Mr Whitney addressed an emergency meeting of the council last night . . . and demanded they cancel your contract on grounds of incompetence . . . sir!'

Kindersley almost smiled. Why, that smug, slimy silvertail! Even so, he interpreted what he was hearing as good news. Whitney's extreme action hinted strongly that Mr Moneybags was coming apart. At last.

He rested a ham on the desk edge and swung his leg.

'And what did our esteemed councillors decide?'

'Voted against the recommendation, Sheriff.'

'So, what are you fretting about?'

'Nothing, Sheriff,' came the quick reply, and the deputy was off like a shot. He'd expected fireworks.

Kindersley moved to occupy the heavy chair at the oak table by the front window. Okay, he might have almost too much to see to today. But right now it felt just fine to sit here in full view of the passers-by and to savor the power, to envision the future almost within his grasp.

They'd removed the sawed-off from the hitch rail by this time and he had an uninterrupted view of the street and vice versa.

By leaning forward just a little and gazing north along Pawnee he could see the cupola of the council chambers building. His lip curled in contempt. Midgets! It was just over a year ago that he had stood before ten of Tarryall's finest to request a modest increase in salary and perquisites, only to be turned down flat. One hundred dollars per month plus fine fees was more than adequate, so heavy-bellied men with bald heads and sweaty dewflaps had informed him. Then, scratching and munching cheese biscuits – town-tame nobodies scared of their wives, enjoying the opportunity to trim this larger-than-life 'hero' down to size – they really slipped the knife in between the short ribs with the reminder that by the time he turned forty-five a town sheriff was considered ready for retirement.

He'd walked into the chambers that day a reasonably committed peace officer, his shadowy past in distant places a vague memory in his own mind. He emerged thirty minutes later the most dangerous man the Nacimientos had ever seen.

That same week High T lost 700 head of Hereford and the sheriff and Stella Whitney got all naked and sweaty for the first time by the light of an outlaw's moon.

He allowed himself a small smile. The amusing part was that the enemy thought they'd had it tough this last year. Kid stuff! The real action was about to unfold.

The sound of boot-heels on porchboards interrupted his daydream. He stared at the familiar figure of the coveralled postmaster in his black-billed cap, then belatedly saw the man was toting a manila envelope.

'What?' he growled, concealing his interest behind a poker face. This man was completely in the sheriff's pocket. He'd caught him pilfering the US mail a long time ago but hadn't lowered the boom on him. There were times when a man like the sheriff needed to transmit and receive messages in secret, and he found the postmaster all too eager to oblige. But this shifty fellow had other attributes, not the least of which happened to be contacts in high places in the county capital.

Undaunted by the sullen greeting, the man placed the envelope upon the table. He was panting because he was out of breath from hurrying all the way from the post office.

'It's come at last, Sheriff,' he whispered raggedly, tapping the envelope. 'Purty overdue, I'll allow. But it's the McCoy, I reckon. That's Pike's hand, and Pike works for the authority.'

'Get out.'

'But, Sheriff. . . .'

'Out!'

He was gone. Kindersley reached for the letter-opener. Today, he was realizing he could treat everybody just how he liked. He was sailing solo; the captain was in command.

The contents of the handwritten letter were brief but very much to the point. One line covered the postmaster's spy's apology for his long delay in securing the information Kindersley sought. The second was even briefer.

It read: 'Confirming Hardy and Birch agents of Bureau as suspected.'

Kindersley sat in the pulsing silence, staring at nothing. For a time he seemed not to breathe. It was just one month since the postmaster's spy had supplied information in return for money to the effect that an internal court hearing in the capital had officially declared the findings in the case of The People vs. Cole Gannon invalid on the grounds of 'contradictory and spurious evidence' further tainted by 'indifferent' handling of the case from the bench by presiding Judge Murdoch. This finding was to be kept secret until a decision was made as to what further course of action might be taken.

This information had spurred Kindersley into a month of high activity during which he'd plotted and hatched and implemented a plan to ensure that Cole Gannon returned to the Sangres.

The plan had worked like a charm. But Gannon had slipped through the sheriff's fingers on Lazy Y, and Kindersley's men were now working overtime to snare him. But the information on Hardy and Birch rang the alarm bells. He must do better, and do it fast. He had no alternative but to believe that Cole Gannon in a witness box before a straight judge could equal a dawn rendezvous with Madam Hemp for the sheriff of Tarryall.

He must find Gannon quickly. And Gannon must die.

A murmur of voices attracted his attention. He folded the letter away and gazed out to see a knot of people gathered directly across the street, facing his window. His scalp pulled tight when he identified the tall and elegant figure of Slater Whitney accompanied by two ranch hands and his son. With them was the all-black figure of the judge who spoke to Whitney before starting across the street, the traffic giving way out of respect.

But there was little respect on hand when Murdoch came clattering into the office on his big walking stick, red-faced and out of breath.

'Yes?' The sheriff was brusque as he rose. There'd been a time when the booze-ridden judge had been important to his plans, even vital. That time was past. 'Keeping kind of fancy company these days, aren't you?'

'This is serious, Sheriff.'

'Tell someone who cares.'

His hand was resting on the doorknob when Murdoch said, 'Mr Whitney is looking for his wife. He . . . er, they want to know if you might be aware of Mrs Whitney's whereabouts?'

The sheriff hesitated, his face unreadable. Then he reefed the door open and stepped outside to stare across the street.

'Lost dogs, lost billfolds and lost wives,' he said loudly, as though speaking to the judge in the doorway, 'they are all the deputies' province. Me? I have more important matters to see to.'

Striding off in the direction of the livery, Kindersley caught a sideways glimpse of young Lonnie struggling in a cowboy's grasp, attempting to come after him. He heard the boy's curse.

The sheriff laughed. They were coming apart and he was growing taller by the hour. He was half tempted to go back and tell that arrogant soon-to-be-ex-rich man where his wife really was.

But of course he didn't. No time for cheap shots or grandstanding on such a vital day.

His boot-heels cracked loudly on the puncheon boards and a long-haired trapper and a massive backwoods timberjack moved smartly from his path.

He didn't even see them; he was looking inward so intently. He saw himself and his great plan in sharp relief, realized the time had come to discard the shrewd and careful methods he'd had to adopt to climb this high. All the grinding legwork was in back of him. Today's events had launched him into battle mode in a way not equalled since he'd strode this street for the very first time with a hundred hellions waiting to test his mettle.

The grave markers of Boot Hill told the result of that campaign in a way no man could query.

Today he had new enemies. He hadn't snared Gannon yet but knew exactly how to do it. His plans for High T were well advanced; that trap was ready to spring. No doubt about that. This too-bright, bogus Indian summer's day would undoubtedly be looked back upon in time and seen in its historical perspective as Kindersley's day.

But there were things he must know before he could be dead sure he could deliver it. Which was why he was heading out of town.

He spent some time in the gloom of the livery waiting for his horse to be readied. Then, sharply conscious of the impressive picture he made astride his high-shouldered bay gelding as he emerged from the dark of the stables into the sunlight, the man who would be king failed to spot the slight figure of Lonnie Whitney turning sharply from the gunsmith's window to glare after him.

'Hey, rich kid,' smirked a grubby youth strutting by. 'Keepin' tabs on your old lady's beau, are you? Hey, hey!'

Lonnie swore viciously and when he looked again the sheriff was gone.

Unaware, Kindersley rode down Pawnee through the traffic, then wheeled off at Diamond and followed it out of town to where the mud of the street slowly gave way to the East Trail.

This road followed the course of Beaver River, moving away from the lowlands and the busy south bridge to climb rapidly where the land rose steeply to form the massive gash in the landscape known as Sheepeater Cliff. A narrow one-horse trail cut down a precipitous section of the hundred-foot high yellowstone cliff face to a fording for those interested in cutting off a couple of miles, and with a taste for danger.

The sheriff wasn't crossing any rivers today. His destination was the highest level of the cliff where stands of heavy oaks and rough-barked Jeffrey pines offered both beauty and privacy, and where a green-topped surrey was drawn up trailside.

The woman sprang down from the rig and ran to greet him as he dismounted. Attired in a beautiful Garibaldi blouse and split riding-skirt and boots of Spanish leather, the rich man's wife looked younger and prettier in the fresh morning, and Kindersley swung her high as a lover should and squeezed her tight the way she liked.

But romance had nothing to do with the business that brought him to this rendezvous today. He'd given Stella Whitney a job to do, and she was proud to demonstrate she had done it very well.

'Slater has shifted virtually all the cattle on to the Bottom Forty, Boyd,' she supplied, a little short of breath. 'I'm sure he fears another attack, as he should. But the punchers are concentrated there with the stock which could make it impossible for Strummer and the boys to raid.'

'They could be otherwise engaged tonight. What else?' He spoke brusquely now he had the information he wanted. The discontented wife and the ambitious lawman had connected almost a year earlier. Throughout their relationship, Stella had been feeding him vital information on such matters as the distribution of ranch stock and the deployment of the hands, especially the nighthawks. This information had made Kindersley's objective to bleed High T white seem almost too easy at times. With the exception, of course, of that time a year ago when everything went awry at Lazy Y. Which reminded him; 'Anything on Gannon?'

'Not a word. But, sugar, I'm not sure Slater mightn't be keeping things from me now. I think he half suspects me . . . even us.' She searched his face anxiously. 'He's very tense behind that top-lofty way of his. I suspect he's near breaking point. Boyd, it wouldn't shock me to discover that he's plotting something to trick you into making a wrong move; to come down on you with all his might. This is not his usual way, as you know, but the man is facing ruin.'

'My heart bleeds, sugar.'

The high mood that had accompanied Kindersley on the journey out had deserted him as he rode away at the trot, leaving his mistress upset and calling after him. He didn't look back. Suddenly he was skinful of doubt, the way he could get whenever his plans weren't going well. When his energy wore thin and he was driven to use violence and cruelty he didn't fully understand.

Nothing new on Gannon; Hardy and Birch now revealed as enemy agents scheming and plotting against him. And now Whitney acting suspiciously, massing his forces close to home on High T and attempting to conceal information from his wife, proof in his eyes that Mr Big had finally come to believe the sheriff was his true and deadly enemy.

All negatives. In bulk.

But as the morning wore on and with the miles to his spread flowing smoothly beneath the gelding's sleek belly, his thoughts and depression lifted. After all, he truly believed he knew how to bag Gannon and put him in the ground. Certainly Hardy and Birch posed a real threat. Yet both they and that sneaky, underhanded government outfit they represented couldn't touch him without Gannon.

So more than ever before, Gannon was the key. And Gannon would surely die. After it was done, the shocked peacekeeper role for him. He could do it well, when required.

The birds were singing. He inhaled the day and felt he was an invincible force riding a brand-new world whose every vista was fresh to his eyes and his for the taking.

9
The Pit

He was ready to ride again.

He stood on the stoop of Chicken Pickles's shotgun cabin, looking up at the vast black valley clouds rolling up over Big Pine Plateau from the east, throwing the rangeland into early gloom.

His rig wasn't that of cowman, cowboy or even drifter. Instead he was enveloped in a shapeless buffalo-robe coat with an ancient, curly-brimmed line-rider's hat tilted low over his face. Deliberately unshaven and unkempt, he considered his disguise adequate to pass anything but the closest scrutiny. And judging by the look of that roiling cloud mass, he could rely upon it to be the darkest of dark nights in Tarryall.

Rawboned Pickles, the long-time friend and fellow cowman who'd been last on his list of folks to visit before heading into town, was impressed by his appearance. He reckoned Gannon looked like the complete range-bum and toughcase except for one thing.

The face.

Sure, a year of hard times with a gun on his hip had changed his former rancher neighbour. But Gannon's face was way too open and honest for him to be taken for anything but the straight-shooter he was. As all of these loosely connected, hard-working men of the land were. And to a man they were for Gannon, anti-Kindersley and pro some huge change in the power structure of Tarryall. If that was worth anything to him.

Gannon felt it was. He had friends to call on if he failed in whatever he planned to achieve in the town tonight; Pickles still wasn't sure just what that was as they shook hands. Maybe Gannon was unsure himself. Just knew he had to see Tarryall, get the feel of it and then assess exactly how to bring Kindersley to justice.

And clear his own name, of course. Don't forget that, fugitive.

'So long, Chick.'

'You take care now, Cole. And, pard, don't, whatever else you might do, don't sell Kindersley short.'

They were all afraid, he reflected, as the grulla carried him towards the trail. All strong and decent men, yet scared of Kindersley where once they'd been merely respectful and wary. They were unanimous that of late the sheriff appeared to have discarded all pretence of compromise and even-handedness to pursue his own ruthless agenda, whatever that might be.

The total cloud cover saw him caught short of his destination in blackness as absolute as the devil's pit. He was relieved when he glimpsed the faint glow of town lights and rode on at a lope, the big horse moving smoothly beneath him and the cold biting his face.

He knew exactly where he was heading after tying up the horse in an empty lot and hitting lower Pawnee. He only hoped the judge wasn't too drunk.

Hat tugged low, he slouched past a group of men lounging along the boardwalk by the Boston Café. They glanced his way then went on talking excitedly; he had no idea what about. I make a good bum, he thought. But he felt more like a warrior as his hand brushed gunbutt beneath the shapeless buffalo hide.

He stiffened as he saw a deputy in a mackinaw coming towards him. But the fellow didn't even give him a glance. The badge looked tense and worried, he thought. Was that a good sign or bad?

An alley took him to the Squat and Gobble where you could buy a crockery cup of lousy sourmash for two bits. Nobody knew Cole Gannon here, and they talked freely enough.

'Kindersley?' The barkeep snorted. They were more scared of the sheriff at the Squat and Gobble than of drunk timberjacks wrecking the joint Saturday nights. 'But don't tell him we said so, stranger.'

'I'm not likely to be talking to the sheriff,' he said, paying his two bits. And hoped this would prove true. This was strictly a scouting mission. Test the waters then decide whether to garner support and tackle Kindersley head-on here, or go to the capital with Hardy and Birch and play out the longer, safer legal game as witness to Gene's murder and the rustling.

From all he'd gleaned during the day he was now convinced Kindersley had been systematically plundering High T for a whole year. And carrying on with Stella Whitney. Crazy? Didn't seem anything crazy about the sheriff to him. But he needed an educated opinion on that one.

Judge Cletus Murdoch all but fell out of his chair in his tiny rat-hole room in back of the courthouse when a tall, buffalo-robed stranger entered, closed the door sharply behind him then jerked off his sorry apology for a hat.

'By the great horned toad of Jerusalem! Gannon? What the pluperfect are you doing here, man?'

'Don't get excited, Judge.'

'Who's excited?' Murdoch croaked excitedly, grabbing up his glass and hurling two ounces of undiluted whiskey down his throat. The liquor gave him strength. 'Damnation and tarnation! It'd be a miserable apology for a judiciary who'd object to a bloody-handed murderer creeping in on him in the dark of the night – ahh, don't hurt me!'

Gannon rested his knuckles on the little table by the big book, level gray eyes staring hard into the ruined face.

'If you start yelling I'll silence you, old man. Otherwise, just shut up and listen. Hear?'

The judge's head bobbed violently. 'I . . . I do believe I know why you're here, young fellow.'

'I could be here to tell you that you tried and convicted me for murder in my absence knowing full well the evidence to be false and the sheriff to be lying in his teeth? Is that your guess . . . Judge Murdoch?'

The judge shook his head wonderingly. He'd been sitting here in solitude with just his bottle and conscience for company, wracked by the most savage pangs of guilt he'd ever experienced in light of an event today of which his visitor had no knowledge. He was certain Gannon had come to him for help. The judge was too afraid to offer help, but for the first time in too long he was at least ready, eager and just drunk enough to want to be honest.

What subsequently transpired before an astonished Cole Gannon in the brief minutes following, was both remarkable and unexpected. For the judge confessed. Not only to the fact that he'd been haunted by the aforementioned trial, which he'd known to be a sham, but, as though in an effort to cleanse himself and demonstrate to this man that he was not all bad, also revealed that it was he personally who'd instigated the investigation by the Territorial Bureau of Investigations at the behest of Slater Whitney.

Whitney also suspected the sheriff s involvement in the rustlings, he blurted out. As did the judge himself. He actually wept a big tear as he poured himself another and explained to his wide-eyed listener how it had been between him and the sheriff. How he'd sat by with his bottle and watched Boyd Kindersley's disintegration from dynamic town-tamer to what he termed 'dangerous megalomaniac' over the period of one long year.

'And do you know what, young shaver?' he summarized dramatically, bug-eyed and weaving as he climbed erect. 'It is far, far from over. Your reappearance, I fear, has galvanized the sheriff into desperate action. You are quite correct in assuming he deliberately drew you back to the county with the intention of destroying you. You gave him the slip and he has been insufferable ever since. He'll stop at nothing to destroy you, as you are doubtless aware.' He shook his head. 'Even I who possibly know him best never believed he'd go this far.'

'This far?'

Murdoch blinked owlishly. 'You mean you don't know? I thought that was what brought you here, man.'

'What are you talking about?'

'Why, the reason I'm drinking, of course. Why Tarryall is hopping mad tonight. He arrested Tessa Dorling this afternoon and is holding her at the law office right now! Bait to lure you to town . . . surely you must have known?'

But Gannon was gone.

Towners paused to stare as they went by. The sight of Sheriff Kindersley taking it easy was an uncommon one. It seemed doubly strange to see their badge-man seated comfortably on the brightly lit front porch of the jailhouse on a cold black night puffing a cheroot and fiddling with what appeared to be a deck of cards.

The jailhouse as always was brightly lit but tonight there was no sign of any deputies, another departure from the usual.

Surely, so they were thinking, the sheriff must be aware of the tensions gripping Pawnee Street tonight in the wake of the arrest of Tessa Dorling?

Didn't he realize folks were good and mad, that everyone was drinking and talking about very little else?

Seemed not.

But appearances could be deceptive, particularly where a man like Kindersley was concerned. In reality the jailhouse was the least relaxed forty squares in Tarryall tonight with all four deputies on full alert and concealed within and Strummer and the sheriff's full ranch crew standing watch from the unlighted upper balcony of the Lucky Deuce opposite.

The sheriff held his fragrant stogy in his left hand as he gusted blue tobacco smoke at the overhead light. His free hand was one inch from gunbutt as he went right on 'relaxing'.

The name of the game: waiting for Gannon. He did not believe the cowman could possibly ignore what he'd done with the Dorling woman. The spider web of deception the sheriff was spinning here tonight was designed to make any would-be Galahad's rescue mission of the damsel in distress appear as simple and easy as swallowing cigar smoke.

Suddenly the front legs of Kindersley's tipped-back chair hit the boards and his right hand wrapped around gunbutt as he belatedly realized that one of the constant stream of passers-by had failed to pass. Indeed the man was leaning against a porch support staring directly at him from a distance of twenty feet, blinking in the light.

Kindersley relaxed and swore softly. It was only the snot-nose. Nothing to worry about there. Except that, he supposed, Lonnie Whitney looked a little less stable than usual, which tallied to highly unstable, by any standard.

'Hi, kid,' he began, but got no further.

From beneath his cream-silk coat Whitney jerked up a nickel-plated pistol and with a muffled curse, jerked trigger.

Town-tamer fast, the big man hit the floor and came up shooting. He shot to disable, and never missed. Lonnie Whitney collapsed clutching his leg and screaming obscenities as men came rushing from all over, deputies, dark figures running from the Deuce, passers-by.

'You keep away from my mother, you lousy, stinking bastard! I'll kill you next time, Kindersley! You hear? Oh, Jesus, get me a doctor. I'm dying – the big bastard's killed me!'

Seemed the only person on Pawnee Street unaffected by the hellish uproar was the man in the centre of it. The sheriff stood impassive and unmoving, six-gun housed, hands on hips, looking more so the giant surrounded by pygmies in that moment when he could feel his entire universe tottering in danger of collapse.

That dopey, crack-brained, daddy-loving rich kid sonuva. . . ! What moronic timing!

It felt almost like the final blow when he sighted the bunch of men who came running into the light from the direction of the mansion, and Kindersley recognized the High T crew with Colonel Whitney at their head.

This meant High T's last remaining big herd was left unguarded, a longed-for situation he could have exploited to the maximum but for one crummy cowman and one idiot kid.

His trigger finger itched as an immediate clash erupted over by the trough between Strummer and a High T puncher. Towners were running to and fro and it seemed about dozens were clustered around the men toting Lonnie off to Doc McTigue's.

It was all running through the sheriff s fingers like quicksilver – until he whipped out a .45 and blew a hole in the sky.

'Shut up and listen!' His voice sounded even louder than the gunshot in the sucked-in silence that followed. He triggered again and the slug smacked ground behind Strummer, and the fighters froze. His commanding glare seemed to find every man in turn as he holstered again and strode out into the middle of the street. And even before he started in laying down the law, everyone, every friend, enemy and undecided was acutely aware that, whatever else they might be unsure of in that electric moment, this was still very much Kindersley's town.

Bust her out now. He'd never get a better chance. But it had to be now. Right now before they either got the street cleared – or all hell broke loose.

Gannon stood there in the dark of the old barn with his eye pressed to a chink in the wall, waiting for some of the trembling to go out of his legs.

He knew he must do it. Would do it. But another must-do in that heart-thudding slice of time was to admit he had never really changed after all. Not really. For a year and more he'd played the part of the hard-bitten fugitive from the law and had at times played the role with some flinty distinction. But this surely was the crucial and the supreme test, even more so than Arroyo's gun hell had been. This was Armageddon stuff for a simple cowman. Attack Kindersley's goddamned armed fortress and somehow get Tessa out of there and make a run for it? That was a task to daunt even a Kindersley. Cole Gannon was never going to be that. Likely nobody was a Kindersley but Kindersley.

'Enough of that, Gannon!' he hissed angrily, and the uncertain moment was passed. It had to be done. He was going to do it. Lonnie Whitney's play had whipped up a fortuitous near-riot in Pawnee, and that must favor his cause, if he just managed to play the right cards from those he'd been dealt.

The gloomy street in back of the law office was deserted now but for the sheriff's lamplit buggy tethered to a snubbing post at the far end of the jailhouse's shadowy rear yard. The grulla stamped a foot nervously in the gloom as shouts arose from Pawnee again. Kindersley had seemed to be gaining control as Gannon had ridden across the main stem a half-block south; now it seemed things might be fixing to bust loose again.

The taut atmosphere reminded Gannon of the eerie hush preceding a blizzard. Tonight, something was happening to Tarryall, the town that had lived, thrived and suffered under an autocrat for maybe too long. He could sense something raw and threatening rising out of the boards and streets as angry men milled and shouted and were afraid and angry all at once. A powder keg? Maybe so or maybe not.

He didn't give a damn one way or another. He was simply solid ready to accept the diversion as a gift from the gods and grab it with both hands.

There was but one deputy visible in back of the jailhouse now, and when Gannon trained his field-glasses on the shady figure he held them on the stocky shape for a long moment before grunting with satisfaction.

A heavy key-ring hung from the man's gunbelt.

There was only one way of going about this and Gannon took it, before his nerve failed him. He was halfway across the street and lurching pretty convincingly before the deputy grew aware of him.

'Hey! Where the hell do you think you're goin'?'

'Got something important to tell you, Deputy,' Gannon slurred, stumbling through the gate. 'Something mighty—'

'Git!' the man reiterated angrily, advancing and gesticulating. 'Who the tarnation are you anyway? Do I know you, bum?'

Gannon stumbled forward, fell to one knee, rose awkwardly as the man reached for him, then struck.

He'd never hit harder or cleaner.

The deputy dropped without a sound and within seconds Gannon was at the solid rear door, fumbling with the keys until one clicked and he was easing inside.

A room lit by three coloured lamps, a passage leading to the cells.

He darted through, keeping low. He could see a section of the front office and the backs of two rifle-toting deputies guarding the windows. The faces of the mob were blurred beneath the streetlights;

someone was shouting angrily about Lonnie Whitney and he heard Tessa's name called by a drunken voice.

Tessa was standing by her barred door as he appeared with the suddenness of a ghost. His finger to his lips was not necessary. The girl stood in silence, her eyes enormous as he jiggled with the keys again. The door swung open. He grabbed her arm.

'What the blue hell! Who's that back there? Hey!'

They were seen.

Gannon reacted like a man who'd been living desperado style all his life. Jerking Tessa past him with one hand, he palmed Colt with the other and crash-blasted two swift shots above the shouting deputies' heads, sending them diving for cover headlong.

'Jailbreak! Jailbreak!'

The hysterical shouts seemed to suck up all other sounds as two lithe figures dashed wildly across the rear yard and over the street to where the grulla stood tied to a tree. Mounting was the work of mere moments yet seemed to take forever. With Tessa clutching his waist, Gannon was urging the big horse forward with a cut of spur, storming eastwards towards the buggy and startling the harness horse, as up ahead two gun-toting figures came rushing down the alley between jailhouse and newspaper office.

Gannon had the shaved tip of a second to identify Kindersley's bulk and Strummer's whipsawed shape. He snapped off a shot at Kindersley but it was lean Strummer who tumbled with a cry of pure agony.

'Gannon!' A sprawled Kindersley identified him

despite his disguise and the dim light. He turned his head and roared over twin gunbarrels: 'You men stay put and quiet the street! He's mine!'

Then the sheriff's Colts crashed and clanged like the great bronze gongs of heaven just as the big mouse-coloured horse swept abreast of the alley-mouth. Cole Gannon drew in a shuddering breath he knew could be his last, then yelled reassuringly, 'It's all right, Tess. Don't be afraid!'

'It's not all right, Cole.' She always had to be right. 'But I'm not afraid.'

He believed her. Only wished he could say the same for himself. If they could just survive the next ten seconds. . . .

10
Winter Kills

The alley-mouth again rocked to the thunder of gunfire as Kindersley loosed another volley of shots, shooting from the hip but shooting as only he could.

The grulla was hit.

Stretched low over the horse's neck with its mane streaming in his face, Tessa clinging to his hips, Gannon groaned as he heard the lead thud home. The horse missed its stride but picked up again to carry them flying by the buggy and black tied up at the corner post.

For a racing moment stretching horse and crouching riders were vividly illuminated in the racing rig's bright running lights.

Six-guns raged behind.

But Kindersley shot high for fear of hitting his own horse, and missed.

He rushed into the street and cut loose again.

Gannon heard slugs dropping harmlessly behind him as a jerk on the reins sent the grulla swerving into the alley leading to Bridge Road.

'You all right?' The slipstream whipped his words away like blown paper.

'Yes,' came the muffled reply. 'But the horse isn't.'

'He'll get us there!'

Gannon's confidence was faked. Charging past the brooding bulk of Ockendon's stables to rush into Bridge, he could hear the animal's laboured breathing. He clapped his hand to its flank and it came away sticky.

They would never make the bridge.

They'd be lucky even to make the risky alternative. Sheepeater Cliff was a good mile from town, and even if he got that far he doubted he could make his way down that one-horse track to the fording in darkness so deep.

He was already thinking in the singular as they hit the rough gravel of the cliff trail and he shot a glance over his shoulder to catch the shimmer of buggy lights flickering the length of Ockendon's unpainted walls.

A faltering horse. A killer with a gun on his tail. No place to run but up that brutal slope. The tally to that equation was all too ugly and plain. He could still easily die. But that rated a poor second to the real fear knotting his guts. For her.

Straightening in the saddle as the grulla began to climb, he hipped around and whipped an encircling arm about Tessa's waist, holding her against him with all his strength for a precious second out of eternity.

Then. 'He's not interested in you, Tess. Never was. He'll keep on after me. That'll give you time. Go see Rory—'

'Cole Gannon!' she cried above the thudding hoofbeats, her face almost invisible in the blackness. 'What are you saying?'

'Ready!' he shouted. With a powerful twist of his body he swung her clear of the horse to hold her suspended kicking and screaming above the blurring trail, then loosed his grip. 'Take care, Tess!'

She hit the earth running and he sensed rather than saw the paleness of her blouse veering off-trail into the brush, her voice raging savagely against it all as he used the spur to go lumbering upward towards the invisible crest. There was zero visibility for a hundred faltering yards. Two. But then there was some light, nothing more than a glow along the trail below and behind, faint at first but strengthening fast as his horse double stepped and began to drop its head.

Another glance backtrail.

The town was lost behind the great trees that barricaded the way to the cliffs. But the 'fiery chariot' that was Kindersley's racing buggy, eating up distance on its rubber-tyred wheels with the crack of the driver's whip sounding like gunshots, was all too vividly visible now.

Gannon wasn't going to make it.

A steely cowman's optimism had kept him on his set course ever since setting out from the Hondo lands. It had seen him survive enough close shaves to turn any cowman's hair white; times when maybe a man with just a modicum of horse sense would up and quit. He'd drawn lavishly on those high hopes and courage he hadn't known he possessed a dozen times. But it seemed like the barrel was bone dry now. Sure he had a gun, and it would be man against man up here in the wind-blown blackness. But he was no kind of gunman, while this ruthless killer closing on him rapidly now as he crested the clifftop and heard the high wind moaning in a grove of Jeffrey pines, was the man who'd faced down the worst hellers in the Sangre de Cristo during his town-taming years, and walked away every time.

'Think of Tessa, Gannon!' an inner voice hissed. And in that moment he was whole again. Strong.

He needed to be.

In mid-stride the brave grulla finally crashed down on its nose. Gannon was expecting it. He sprang clear, seeming to float in blackness for breathless moments before slamming sideways against solid ground. He shoulder-rolled to his feet only to be immediately smashed full length with an incredible weight rolling over him like the night had collapsed upon him.

Agonized, barely conscious, he realized the horse had struggled back on to its feet then crashed blindly into him, bringing them both down yet again. This time the horse didn't rise.

Spitting blood and fumbling for his shooter, Gannon forced himself away from the thrashing animal as yellow light flooded the trail, causing the pines to leap from the darkness on either side. He propped himself up on one arm, clutching the six-gun. Kindersley was bearing down on him like some Apocalyptic vision, standing in the rig now, driving one-handed with the other hand spewing crimson gunflame. Raging.

Gannon was hit.

Surely only a Kindersley could hit a target from a moving platform under such conditions! Sent rolling by the brutal impact of the bullet, Gannon cursed and locked his jaws against his pain to somehow get on to his knees and bring the gun up to eye level.

One shot.

Was that all he'd get time for?

He wouldn't bank on a second as a screaming slug tugged at his shirtsleeve and the charging buggy horse assumed the dimensions and menace of a runaway locomotive in the fugitive's blurring vision.

He squeezed trigger.

It was like viewing a lantern-slide in slow frames as the horse buckled in the traces, the lamplit buggy rising up spectacularly behind it to seemingly stand on its shafts as the limbs-flailing, flying creature that was the driver flew high, briefly underlit by gaudy lamplight in the split second before man, horse and rig came crashing back to earth with a sound like a coffer dam breaking up at thirty below.

A heavy object from the rig struck Gannon's shoulder. He didn't even feel it through his pain. His right leg was soaked in blood as he tried to crawl out of harm's away. For a moment he had the crazy hope that all the lamps had been smashed in the wreck. No such luck. One light survived. It was barely feet from where he lay. It flickered wanly against the ground as the echoes of the crash subsided. Then the glow seemed to be strengthening as, from somewhere close by in the semi-darkness he heard a snarl of pure rage and a moment later the apparition rose up from the wreckage, eyes blazing in the uncertain light.

Kindersley's jacket was half ripped off and flapping in the wind. His bloodied hands were empty as he came lunging over the splintered dashboard like some wild animal beyond anything but fury.

'I should have finished you in Arroyo, sodbuster!' he said thickly, and Gannon barely had time to struggle erect before this seeming giant was rushing in.

He side-stepped somehow. They circled.

'Give up, man,' Gannon urged, spitting blood. 'Hardy and Birch are government agents, don't you understand? The authorities know everything – about the rustling, your murdering Gene and framing me everything. We all know.'

'They might think they know things, but they can prove nothing without you, hick. And I'll still get it all. The High T, the wife, the big house. I'll wallow in it, sodbuster, while you'll be nothing but dust.'

Anger knotted Gannon's guts.

'Then if you won't turn yourself in, I'll finish you, just the way you did Gene!' And he smashed a vicious right to the sheriff's head.

Kindersley was fifty pounds heavier and knew every roughhouse trick in the book. That was a given. But Gannon felt a rush of adrenaline as they came violently together. For whether it was rage, cussedness or simple desperation that fuelled him now, suddenly he was devoid of all weakness and was only conscious of an exhilarating sensation of righteous power, as though he were the last man standing against the evil of the world.

They heaved each other about viciously, never breaking their death-grips, stumbling and crashing back and forth amongst the wreckage, knees pistoning for vitals, clawing at eyes and throats, feeling maniacally for the kill. Two men with their clothing ripped apart and smeared in blood. Two men who. had hated so long they were reduced to the level of beasts. Kill or be killed.

Gannon made the first mistake. He trod on a dropped gun and stooped to pick it up. A swinging forearm caught the side of his head and drove him several feet to crash violently against the buckled and twisted wreckage of the buggy. As he made to rise through a red mist of agony, he saw Kindersley coming up with the .45 in his fist, teeth locked in a grimace of ultimate triumph.

Gannon realized his leg lay against the lamp. He kicked out with all his strength. Glass burst and the light snuffed as he hurled himself full length beneath the screaming slug that furrowed his back.

The gunflash died and someone was groaning like a sinner in torment.

Kindersley is running.

God knows he shouldn't be. Not up here in the black void of the clifftop trail. But he can't stop as he blunders blindly into objects which seem to reach out and claw at him, the blackness laying traps he stumbles into, the sudden lash of pain as he runs into a tree.

And now he is down with the sound of his own breath roaring in his ears. Where is Gannon? Where is the cellar door? Where the light?

It is so long since he's known total darkness that it seems impossible, even to his befuddled senses, that he could be transported back so swiftly over so many adult years to the boy, the storm cellar, the brutal father.

'Please let me out. Please, oh please!'

'You'll stay in there under lock and key until you learn respect, you little varmint. Forever, if that's what it takes.'

And it had seemed like forever. As it did now. Instant foreverness encompassed by eternal night. He'd killed his father seventeen times since the terror stopped; but the terror never died.

And he groans aloud as the compressed pain in his chest spreads wider still and the ringing in his ears brings him to his feet again to hear himself call: 'Gannon! Make a light and we'll talk. Please, Gannon? Gannon, you motherless scum!'

He rages. And his words whirl like leaves in a dead-cold merciless winter's wind.

But the rage will not last. Not against the terror it won't. Is that the old man's mocking laughter? He fights for reason. He must be facing north. Yes, he is sure he can feel the north wind against his face. The cliff is south. At his back. He starts forward. He stops. The doubt.

Is the cellar door really this way . . . or over yonder?

'Please, papa.'

He can not breathe. The sheriff lies staked upon the altar of the demons of darkness. But he is up again. Isn't he? He fights against panic. He tries to ignore the taste of dirty copper that lies under his tongue. He tries again to suppress his whimpering, which reaches but faintly the ears of the silent man seated motionless upon a boulder some distance away, barely seeming to breathe; just listening now.

With his senses deserting him, sucking for oxygen, the sheriff makes one last heroic struggle to gauge direction, to place himself in this inky pit.

North wind blowing. Surely it is that against his face. North lies the town. He can make it back if he can but breathe.

The sheriff is walking. He runs. Runs in the direction he knows the lights will soon appear – the blessed benediction of the lights. He runs faster and there are no obstructions reaching for him now. He will soon be out of this pit as huge as the world, his heavy boots crunching gravel.

Then empty air.

He is plummeting through a blackness deeper than anything man or God could ever conceive. Beyond imagining. Beyond nightmare. Down the last dark pit of all.

The sound of a heavy body striking solid rock one hundred feet below reaches Gannon like the whisper of a falling snowflake.

The post-mortem became necessary only when doctor and undertaker failed to agree on the exact cause of death. The shattered corpse had not bled as it should have, so the medic insisted. The examination was thorough and by the time it was through both men were in full agreement as to the cause of death. Heart failure. The lawman's perfectly healthy heart had failed before his body was dashed to pieces upon the iron toe of Sheepeater Cliff.

Near as they could diagnose, Boyd Kindersley had died of fright.

Standing side by side and shackled to the iron rail affixed to the sturdy side wall of the railed-off bench chamber which occupied one third of Tarryall courthouse, the prisoners appeared ugly, fearful and still dangerous enough to satisfy even the least impressionable of the capacity house.

The Kindersley Ranch 'crew' was not widely known in Tarryall. They kept to themselves, and if even half the rumors, whispers, allegations and newspaper reports circulating through town concerning their involvement in capital crimes were true, then the town was fortunate that this had been the case.

There was the so-called wrangler, with the sour, cruel features of a genuine owlhoot – or so the spectators were ready to believe. He stood glowering next to a runt with a mean and twisted little face, then a hairy Hercules with the look of a braggart and a blowhard, a beanpole with yellow eyes and the wild-eyed kid who'd suffered a broken arm in the ruckus at the jailhouse with High T.

It had been the judge's idea to put Kindersley's cattle-rustling gang on display today. With the sheriff in his grave and so many questions as yet unanswered, despite four days of hectic activity at lawhouse and jail by everyone from the judge and the legal heavyweights from the plains down to the deputies and even the man in the street, Murdoch felt the people wanted some tangible evidence of progress in the case for the people to focus on.

Right now, even before the citizens' hearing got under way, there were those amongst the outraged community ready to tar and feather anyone connected with Kindersley and all his perceived crimes.

The shackled prisoners had four deputies on hand to ensure their safety, although it was highly unlikely there would be any trouble. For one thing, the judge had always maintained great authority and control in his courtroom. But the reality was that even the most outraged towner present was far more interested in just sitting quietly and soaking up the sworn truth today than raising hell.

Few had a real grasp of the true extent of crime and corruption in Fall River County as yet, which was the principal reason the judge had arranged this hearing-cum-exposé. It would be some time before formal charges would be made and sworn evidence taken. It was both Murdoch's opinion and that of his superiors that a community that had been through so much should not have to be kept in the dark any longer than was already the case.

Apart from that, all the legal heavyweights present, and Murdoch himself, were themselves eager to see and hear what the day might throw up. There were any number of burning questions to which there were as yet no answers.

'The court will rise!'

The clerk's sudden shout brought a packed house to its feet and the tall oak doors in back of the bench were opened and Murdoch came through in a swirl of black robes, pince-nez perched on his generous nose. Square-jawed and purposeful, documents tucked beneath one arm and pink of cheek and healthy of eye, plainly the judge appeared sober – first shock of the big day.

Murdoch stood before them clutching his 'Bible'.

'By the authority invested in me by God and the Great and Honourable territory of New Mexico I hereby proclaim this Public Judicial Meeting of the Twenty-third District Court open. The first purpose of this said meeting being to establish certain facts, gather evidence and listen to all testimony which may be available. But the second and more important reason is to still civic disquiet and to reveal to you, our esteemed citizenry, all known facts and conclusions arrived at thus far in relationship to recent cataclysmic events. Be seated!'

Tarryall lay axle-deep in snow that morning, the long-awaited blizzard having raged for the past thirty-six hours. The weather had no effect upon attendances at the courthouse, however. The building could accommodate 150, but due to the numbers wanting to get in, the officials permitted another fifty standing, then had the deputies close the doors.

Gannon was feeling pretty chipper for a man with sixteen stitches in his leg and a heavily bandaged ankle, as he sat quietly with the Dorlings up front by the jury box.

How the rest of Tarryall felt that marrow-freezing morning as the judge welcomed them all to sit in on this historic event, was less clear. Maybe the judge could help them understand more clearly exactly what infamy had apparently been taking place under their very noses for so long. Throw some light on why and how their town had almost erupted into chaos Friday night. Tell them what he knew about the sheriff.

It wasn't too long before a suppressed buzzing washed through the tightly packed galleries, with neighbour looking at neighbour in growing surprise.

The judge wasn't slurring. His complexion seemed an almost healthy pink in contrast to its customary whiskey-red. He was articulate. Nobody had really believed he'd arrived sober, even though he looked it. But by this it was growing plain he was straight as Carrie Nation today. So they supposed he had some right to sound just a tad proud and boastful as he made it perfectly clear for the record that the man most responsible for all the good things which had emerged from the ruins of Fall River County's murky year, was Cletus J. Murdoch.

'As well, of course,' he had the grace to add, 'our own redoubtable brother and standard-bearer for righteousness, Mr Cole Gannon.'

You could hear a pin drop as proceedings got under way, with the judge grabbing their full attention right off by revealing how Colonel Whitney had come to him in desperation concerning the numerous rustling raids on his ranch.

Already suspicious, Whitney had begged the judge to keep his request confidential; under no circumstance was the sheriff to know of it. For reasons of his own – namely fear of his fellow lawman – Murdoch agreed. He had professional contacts in a low profile investigative body in the capital, he explained now, and they in turn had proceeded to launch a detailed investigation into events in the county over the past year with emphasis on the Dorling–Gannon–Kindersley affair at Lazy Y.

The room buzzed as Murdoch donned his pincenez to read the official report handed down, based on examinations of the transmission of the *in absentia* trial of Cole Gannon, accused of Gene Dorling's death. They even began to cheer in some quarters when it was made clear that, in the view of this august arm of the Supreme Court, that trial had been flawed and corrupt, its findings insupportable.

The judge beamed. But there was always one in any crowd. 'Hey, didn't you preside over that there trial yourself, Murdoch?'

'The judge is not on trial here,' said the silver-haired circuit judge, sent up from the capital to assist today's hearing, rising from his chair. 'You all should know that what is patently plain from the information collated over the past few days is that the late Sheriff Kindersley presided over a systematic rustling operation over a long period of time and stands accused posthumously of both initiating the shooting of Gene Dorling and falsely accusing Mr Gannon for that crime.'

The speaker gave them a moment to absorb this bald declaration which came as no shock to a handful, but plainly stunned many.

Then Murdoch announced gravely; 'Deputies, bring in our volunteer witness.'

Stella Whitney took the stand and the judge was obliged to work overtime with his gavel to quell the uproar before motioning to the pale but composed woman to please say her piece.

Turned out that the shooting of her son had affected Stella Whitney profoundly, so much so that she had approached the law with a story to tell. She proceeded to tell it again now without hesitation despite having been warned beforehand just how serious what she had to say could be for her.

Stella Whitney was past fretting about Stella Whitney. She'd sinned and now sought absolution at any price. From her son, her husband, the people of the county, perhaps even from God himself. She would take what she could get as she knew she had most likely lost just about everything else.

The ugly story she related was short and unembellished. A discontented wife had struck back at boredom and resentment of her husband's parsimony by entering a romantic alliance with a man of towering ambition.

'Yes,' she attested soberly, 'to all you good people who spent so much time wondering and repeating whispers, Boyd Kindersley and I were lovers.'

It was some time before Murdoch could restore quiet. The crowd was getting its money's worth.

She continued; Kindersley wanted the High T and convinced Stella they could take it over one day and share it together by the 'simple' expedient of his rustling gang, headed up by Strummer, attacking the rich man's herds, with her supplying all the internal information necessary to ensure the successful outcome of such an operation.

She confessed she'd been 'horrified' by the shooting of Gene Dorling but had allowed herself to be convinced by Kindersley that Strummer had done the killing on his own initiative.

'I always allowed Boyd to talk me round,' she confessed, touching a lace handkerchief to the corners of her eyes now. 'I'm sure everyone who knew him would understand how easy that was to do. I thought I knew everything about Boyd but I guess I knew nothing. Why, I didn't even know he was afraid of the dark. I . . . I may have gone on believing everything he told me until we'd finally won our dirty fight and the High T was ours, but for what happened with my son . . . my precious son.'

She gazed down upon Whitney and Lonnie. They were seated together. The pale boy's arm was swathed in a black silk sling. She made a whispered plea for their forgiveness before leaving the dock.

Next, Hardy and Birch presented their version of events, followed by a learned legal gentleman associated with the Bureau offering his slant on recent events. After which a reluctant Cole Gannon limped into the witness box to offer a terse but gripping account of the sequence of violent events on the night the sheriff died.

Some at the back tried to get a cheer going when he described how he'd sat quietly in the dark, hurt and unarmed, listening as Kindersley blundered his way into eternity like some great sightless animal beset by primitive terrors. But Judge Murdoch, who'd actually been sober three full days and was vowing to stay that way now he'd recovered his self-respect, quickly secured order.

Then: 'You must surely be wondering at the absence of one Mr Strummer, who would appear to be central to this enquiry, ladies and gentlemen. Deputy, if you would be so good.'

A deputy went out and returned leading a manacled Strummer. The man was scarcely recognizable. Gannon's bullet had nearly finished him. But he'd recovered to find himself accused number one in Kindersley's absence, an unenviable position, which, so the judge had made clear to him, would assuredly lead him to the gallows unless Strummer was prepared to turn territory's evidence and furnish the many details which the authorities needed to flesh out their investigation.

Strummer sang like a bird on the promise he might draw ninety-nine years instead of the rope.

He sang again for this packed house. For one brutal year Kindersley and Strummer had played the game hard all the way in Fall River County. Yet in their fall, each had revealed the soft underbelly of the weakling.

It was Strummer who held the crowd spellbound with details of the Gannon affair. When a spy informed Kindersley of the secret legal findings regarding the Dorling killing – and that the long-gone Gannon could easily get them both hanged should he be located – Kindersley had immediately decided he must draw Gannon back to Tarryall and kill him before he could be found and testify against him.

The postmaster was in the gallery as Strummer revealed how he'd revealed details of Tessa Dorling's correspondence with the fugitive. This inspired Kindersley's ploy to attack the Lazy Y and thereby lure Gannon.

On hearing this, a man promptly punched the postmaster in the head and a deputy went up the tiers to break it up and arrest the man for interfering with the US Mail.

It was coming to a close. But a now almost humble Murdoch had a confession to make.

'I take no pride, fellow citizens, in admitting that I had sensed for a long time that the sheriff could well be involved in something criminal. I knew him well . . . I was even aware of his darkness phobia. So, why didn't I do anything about this for so long? Simple. I was afraid. I think we all of us started out being admiring of Boyd Kindersley, and then grew afraid. Let us hope that next time, if there ever is one, we might have greater courage.'

It ended soon after that.

Filing from the big white building into the frigid day with the Dorlings, Gannon was startled when someone clapped him on the shoulder and another hollered, 'Let's hear it for Cole Gannon! This man has been through sheer hell, and iffen he hadn't dast come back to take the sheriff on he might've broke us all in time. Cole Gannon, folks!'

Another man might have welcomed the acclaim which erupted around them as the three made their way across to the wagon yard. Not him. He didn't see himself as any kind of hero. Just a man who'd been given a second chance and was eager to seize it with both hands.

Patch up the south yard fence knocked over by the blizzard. Get the rest of the cows in before they froze to death. Chop enough firewood to last at least a month then see to the leak in the kitchen roof. Easy when you said it quick.

There was no shortage of chores on the Lazy Y. But Gannon had identified them all and had already reached the wood-chopping phase, despite warnings about his health from the doctor, Tessa and 'most everybody who happened by.

Another week here then maybe he could head back to the Whetstone and get busy hunting wild cattle in the snowy canyons to start his herd again, From scratch. Just as he'd done five years ago.

He wasn't complaining.

He even managed a grin as he heard voices raised in argument drifting from the house. Tessa and the old man at it again. Everything normal as blueberry pie on Lazy Y.

He'd hauled the logs into the yard with the mule then fixed up the old bucksaw with the home-made frame and rawhide thong tightener.

He sawed up the logs first then split them with the axe and piled them into the shed. Above the racket he was raising he didn't hear Tessa's approach in the deep snow. But she made her presence known, as was her way.

'If you burst those stitches, Cole Gannon, it will be your own fault.'

He paused with the axe slanted across his body, sweating and grinning. 'They're my stitches, Tess.'

She flushed. She was dressed as usual in Gene's working clothes, Levis, sheepskin, hair as black as pitch against the snowy backdrop.

'Do you want gravy with your venison? I've been calling from the porch.'

'Speckled gravy or marble gravy?'

She spun on her heel. She acted mad. She mostly

was. He set the axe aside and stopped grinning. 'Tess!' His voice was sharp.

She propped without turning. 'What now?'

Gannon had done some dangerous and damnfool things over the past year. But nothing seemed half as chancy as what he was going to do now. What he'd ached to do for so long.

He went to her and seized her roughly by the arm. She whirled angrily and her eyes blazed at him. He imprisoned her other arm and, dragging her resisting body hard against his own, kissed her fully on the mouth. She fought and he kissed her harder still, until she wasn't fighting any longer, but kissing him back just the way he'd dreamed she one day might, until it was safe to release her even if she didn't seem to want that now.

'That,' he said simply. He had finally carried out the most important duty he had assigned himself here. It beat the hell out of all the other chores for the way it made this lonely man feel.

They had kissed before. But never like this.

'What. . . ?' she said in bewilderment after a long moment.

'It's over,' he said with a steely look in his eye.

'What is?'

'Your playing at rancher.' Quiet Cole Gannon was suddenly masterful as his sweeping gesture encompassed the tumbledown acres. 'You've been doing a man's work so long you've gotten to forget what you are. I'm back. I'm the man around here now, and there's only room for one.'

She looked ready to erupt. 'And what does that make me?'

'The woman who's going to cook and sew and cook my breakfast and wear gingham, by God.' He pressed his finger to her lips, hard. His voice was still strong yet softer now as he stared into her brilliant eyes. 'The woman I'm going to marry come spring and make happy for the rest of her life.' He stepped back. 'Now get busy with that gravy. But change out of those pants first.'

Who would dare fling nitro into the maw of a restive volcano? Quiet Cole Gannon was who. Tessa Dorling was breathing angry fog gusts into the frigid air as she strode for the house. But by the time she'd mounted the stoop and turned, a miracle had taken place. It was a pretty blushing young woman with actual tears in her eyes who gazed back tenderly at the man swinging the axe.

She had never wanted to be a man. She had become what life had made her, just like him. Yet now, memories of the years of hardship and grinding responsibility vanished like woodsmoke as she allowed herself to see Tessa Dorling as she really was. And all she had ever wanted was to love and be loved by this man and be the woman he wanted her to be.

To care for him by day and love him every night. To nurse his baby to her breast by the silvery morning light.